A Dusty Tale

by

Sue Tinder

"A Dusty Tale" by Sue Tinder

ISBN: 978-0-6151-4015-5

This book is dedicated to
children everywhere;
from the youngest in age to
the most senior among us.

Introduction

Come, sit a spell, relax, and enjoy as you venture on a most remarkable and fascinating tale.

This heart-warming story centers on one typical, modern day New England family of four and their truly unexpected, extraordinary experience.

Their journey of discovery begins with the revelation of their inheritance, a cleaning fairy.

A dense fog begins to lift in the early morning hours in this section of the New England coastline. As the fog rolls back into the vast emptiness from which it came, a stately centuries old private college is revealed.

The main buildings of this fine institution have remained relatively unchanged over the many decades which have passed since it was built. Flanked on the one side by the rugged coastline and on the other by a small community, modern society has been, for the most part, kept at bay.

The grounds of the college begin to bustle with the activity of arriving students and faculty entering the campus at the start of yet another day. One of the faculty members is a psychology professor, Dave Sams.

This institution has been Dave Sams' employer since his own graduation from its halls almost twenty years ago. And, yet, for the first time in all these years, every step he takes this morning brings another memory. Each one is as fresh as though it has just occurred, like that hundred plus year-old tree he passes on the grounds next to the stone steps.

That tree was where he proposed to his wife, Dorrie, more than a dozen years ago. Like all those who came before them, they followed in the tradition of carving their initials in its trunk. Dave smiles slightly.

He and Dorrie grew up in the small town nearby where everyone is close and everyone knows everyone. The pair only lived a few houses apart. People, including their family and friends, took for granted that some day when they were of age; they would marry and raise a family of their own here. The good citizens in this community were right. A month later, they took their wedding vows.

Dave's smile transitions into a frown. It is not because of the memories. Dave and Dorrie have created many a remarkable memory. Instead, his frown stems from the difficulties the couple has experienced over the last several months and primarily last week. He tries very hard to mask his feelings but it is hard, very hard.

Problems, difficulties, whatever term one wishes to use are a fact of life as one ages. It is just a cold, hard fact of life. Some of these changes evolve around are life altering events that are never easy or pleasant to deal with. Take for example the death of a life one.

The Sams' household was rocked not that many days ago when Dorrie's grandmother passed away. Her passing has been hard not only on Dorrie, but also on him. She was far more to him than an in-law. She was closer to him than his own family. Grams, as she was known, was a very special woman.

Dave dearly loved her. Maybe it was because she never fit the stereo-typical version of an in-law. Grams, from the moment he met her, always treated him as if he were one of her own children. Fact of the matter was, there were times it seemed to him that she treated him better than her own flesh and blood.

He smiles on the inside reflecting back to the moment he and Dorrie had told her they were getting married. Her classic response was, "Well, of course you are. I wouldn't have it any other way."

Dave exhales. This is his first day back to the campus since Grams' death. He had taken the maximum number of allowed days for bereavement leave. Dorrie needed those days as did he.

He blinks. So far his return to work has been nothing much more than a mindless blur filled with memories. It has been a haze of sorts occasionally interrupted by passing faculty and students and their chattering amongst themselves.

Typically Dave's ascent up the decades old, granite steps comes with great ease. He can make it from the car through the school's front doors in less than five minutes. Instead, today, it is slow and tedious and he is finding each successive step just as difficult as the first.

Grams had been ill for several years. Three months ago, after Grams medical checkup, the doctors had informed Dave and Dorrie that her condition was rapidly deteriorating. Those few, precious months were probably the most painful ones Dave and his wife have ever known.

Grams had given her doctors specific orders not to tell the couple. The doctors, on the other hand, violated their patient's request and shared her diagnosis. They felt that it would be inhumane to do otherwise. All loved ones should be given the opportunity to create good memories with whatever time a person has left.

Dave and Dorrie mustered themselves up to meet the challenge. They moved into Grams' house to help her care for it and so the two could spend more quality time with her. Both are quite appreciative of the doctors' confiding in them.

Now, Dave and Dorrie must go about with the business of living. It is an easier task for Dave than for Dorrie. Dorrie was raised by Grams after Dorrie's parents were killed in an airplane crash. She was only two at the time and has little to no memory of her parents.

Everything regarding blood family for Dorrie centered on Grams. She was the woman who took Dorrie to her first day of school, taught her the alphabet, was behind the camera for every birthday, and who was present at their wedding.

Grams left the house, everything she had, for Dorrie and her family. It was her wish that they enjoy her home. And, so the couple still lives in her house with all of her furniture, pictures, and most of all memories.

Dorrie is having difficulty coping. It is all still too fresh, too new. And, because of it, Dave is expending greater and greater effort helping her.

Dave is so deep in thought as he approaches the school's main doors that he has not been acknowledging the many "hellos" that have come his way. Generally speaking he is one of the first to bid others good morning.

It is just his luck this morning that one of his young, female students by the name of Beth Grissom (a most obnoxious individual) has kept a watchful eye out for the professor. She had heard he was due back to the campus today and she has every intention of talking to him.

What she has to say to him is very important. At least she feels the subject matter is something she should share with him. The first order of business is to get his attention. This will not be as easy as usual.

Beth parts with the two students she has been walking with. "Gotta go," is all she said to them before racing across the lawn to the steps.

"Hey, Professor Sams. Professor Sams," Beth calls waving her arm.

The two students chuckle at Beth. "She is on another mission," says the one.

"Pity her target," says the other.

Dave does not hear her at first. And, Beth, being Beth is most undaunted in her pursuit. She continues to yell and wave her arms. There is no way even Dave in his current state can not hear her.

Dave finally hears her voice above all the other voices surrounding him. He tries very hard to ignore her hoping that perhaps she is calling to another professor. But, to his chagrin that is not the case.

It is not that he does not like Beth. That has nothing to do with it. For one thing, he is having enough difficulty just being on campus today without having to add an ingredient like Beth to the mix.

Beth is an above average student in intelligence and never misses a class. But, on the downside she is a bit, well to be polite, she is a bit out there. It is his opinion and some of the other faculty members that Beth would make for a good study of the paranormal.

Just as she is about to quit her pursuit, she tries one last time and is able to muster a very strong yell. "Professor Sams!"

There is volume and determination in her voice that Dave will soon be unable to ignore. He continues to walk up the steps under the gaze of students and faculty alike. They are all beginning to stare at him.

Beth is not dissuaded. She believes herself to be on a very important mission; one which can help him and his wife. He has always been one of her favorite instructors and, in her opinion, open to a student's ideas.

She crosses the courtyard's well manicured lawn and up the steps in record time. His lack of response to her leaves her feeling that she has no other choice than to physically intercept him.

Dave is just a few steps shy of the campus' main doors when he suddenly feels a tug on his arm. He does not want to look and see who it is because he is pretty sure it is Beth. Her eccentricity is something he believes he cannot deal with today.

Another, stronger tug is felt on his arm. He responds with a mere turn of his head. To his chagrin it is Beth. Dave immediately steps forward.

Beth's hand loosens its light grip of Dave's arm. She looks at her hand a moment in disbelief then scurries to catch up to him and keep pace.

"Professor, Professor Sams," she calls approaching him yet again.

Dave does not break stride.

Winded, Beth struggles to keep up with his long strides. "Professor," she almost pleads.

Dave finally stops. "Yes?" he asks without as much as a glance in her direction.

"Professor," she abruptly steps directly in his path.

Dave is left with no choice other than to finally concede to her persistence, "Yes, Beth?"

Beth catches her breath, "Sorry to hear about your mother-in-law."

Dave responds in a solemn voice that she can barely hear. "Thank you for the card and flowers." He cannot believe she hurried so just to say this.

"You're welcome. Good to see you back at school," she offers.

Dave forces himself to muster a smile as slight as it may be. He lies to her when he responds with, "Good to be here."

Heaven knows that deep down he would much rather be at home helping Dorrie through all the stages of grief she faces. Not around a group of alleged adults who treat the collegiate learning environment like a super-sized social club.

A moment of silence passes between them leading Dave to believe that Beth has said her piece. But, the student does not move. So, he nods slightly and takes a side step forward. Beth steps in concert.

"Was there something else, Beth?" he asks her hoping she goes about her way.

Beth stutters a bit. She feels a little embarrassed at not only confronting him in such a manner but also with the subject matter. He is a psychology professor after all.

A long, awkward moment passes before she tells him, "After my father passed away I found a lot of comfort through, um, by going..."

Dave looks at his watch impatiently. "Just blurt it out and get it over with," he thinks to himself.

Beth looks at the school doors and then at Dave, "Oh, yes, right, mustn't make the professor late.

Dave nods and gazes at the school's doors.

Passing students wave at the pair. Beth and Dave wave in return.

"Well," she stammers. "What I was going to say is, I found a lot of comfort going to Mother Séance.

"Who?" he asks his interest somewhat piqued.

Beth stops rambling and gets to the point, "I'm going to a séance this evening if you and Mrs. Sams would like to come."

Dave's eyes narrow.

"I know you teach psychology but I just thought..."

He quickly interrupts cutting her off. "No, thank you."

Dave quickly brushes past the student. But, his skirting of Beth is not a strong enough deterrent. For Beth deftly and quickly passes a business card to him.

The young woman then immediately disappears. She blends into the throng of students entering the building before Dave has a chance to grasp what has just occurred.

He is stunned at Beth's actions and it is a slow moment before he glances at the card. "Maybe this is why you are having so many problems in class. Unbelievable. A séance," he shakes his head.

At home, the well manicured exterior of the Sams' 1880's residence gives no clue as the total mess that lies within its four walls. One can gather the state of the rest of the house within a few feet of the front door.

It is in a chaotic disarray of scattered toys, books, and newspapers littering the rooms. Dishes are piled high in the kitchen sink. Opened bags of chips and cookies sit on the counter. Empty food containers litter the counter and the large trash can overflows.

Dave's beloved Dorrie looks aged beyond her thirty years. Her eyes are swollen from the many tears she has shed over the loss of Grams. Her motivation for doing even the simplest of tasks have all but evaporated these last few weeks.

Dorrie stands in the kitchen. She came in here to take care of something. But, now that she is in here, she does not remember what it was. She looks around at all the little knick knacks Grams had collected.

"Grams, you were the only real mother I ever knew. You reared me. You taught me. I was only two when my parents died in that airplane crash. What am I going to do without you," Dorrie's eyes tear up. "You were my best friend."

Dorrie leans against the refrigerator a moment feeling her strength having left her. She grabs a paper towel and wipes her eyes and blows her nose.

Dorrie leaves the kitchen and walks ever so slowly up the stairs to the attic. This was a very special room for her as a child. Grams had said that only the two of them knew of this "secret" room. It was there that the two played for hours.

She passes by the many decades old, black and white, family photographs that fill the walls of the staircase. Her hand reaches out tenderly touching the last one. It is a photo of Grams taken at her eightieth birthday party a mere three months ago. Dorrie sighs.

A world of memories overwhelms Dorrie the moment she opens the attic door. The room is filled with boxes of Gram's personal effects, Dorrie's toys from childhood, and old furniture including a dresser situated along the one wall.

A darkened corner of the room catches Dorrie's eye. She picks up a furniture pad from the floor and walks over to the corner. There, a large, wood doll house stands in the same spot as it has for years. She carefully covers it with the furniture pad.

"Your father made this for you, Grams, when you were just five years-old. He made every piece by hand," she hangs her head and turns away. "There were no power tools back then were there?"

Dorrie passes through a ray of light emanating from the room's lone window. She opens it to air out the strong mothball odor of the room.

Turning from the window, her eyes come to rest on the cedar chest in the middle of the room. Dorrie's eyes mist. She approaches the cedar chest and kneels next to it. Her hand carefully, thoughtfully strokes the lid, "I miss you, Grams."

Dorrie brushes the light coating of dust off the top of the chest with her hands and then opens it. Inside are four quilts Grams made as a young married woman. Even though they were used regularly until her illness some nine years back, they still look brand new, none the worse for wear. She strokes the top one tenderly then touches it to her cheek.

A faint glow suddenly radiates from the inside of the chest. Startled, Dorrie drops the quilts on the floor not noticing a folded piece of paper which separates from the quilts and flutters to the floor. Her eyes fixate on the chest.

Dorrie sits motionless for a moment in a mesmerized state created by the chest's interior glow. It increases in intensity with each passing moment.

"What the?" Dorrie rubs her eyes thinking that she is surely seeing things. But, no amount of rubbing, blinking, even shaking her head makes the light go away. So, Dorrie cautiously leans in toward the chest to take a closer look.

To her amazement she discovers a large, mason jar in the bottom of the chest. It had been concealed by the quilts. The jar glows with an unusual brilliance as Dorrie draws closer. A brilliance the likes of which Dorrie has never seen before. Not even the sun in rising or setting is close to the hues the jar is emitting. The sight of such an indescribable light leaves her momentarily breathless.

Dorrie tentatively touches the jar not once or twice but three times before deciding to remove it from the chest. She carefully picks it up with both hands. Its size is deceptive of its weight. The jar is far heavier than she anticipates.

"What are you made of lead?" she asks holding the jar in front of her eyes. And, then, something else unexpected occurs. The jar's glow flares like a starburst.

The light momentarily blinds Dorrie. She gasps and loses her hold on the jar. It drops to the floor without breaking and rolls several inches away.

"Ouch!" a tiny, feminine voice yells out as the jar hits the floor.

"Huh?" Dorrie looks around the room expecting to see someone. She listens a bit and does not hear anything. "How silly," she thinks of herself. "There is no one in the attic but me." Yet, she still finds herself looking behind her.

Dorrie takes a relaxing breath then reaches out and picks up the jar. Its light has gone out and it is just another dark amber mason jar. She studies it a moment.

"Why would Grams hide you in the chest? Is there a treasure inside?" she smiles slightly then twists hard to open the lid.

A little more elbow grease and Dorrie is able to get it open. At that instant a little light flies out startling Dorrie. She gasps and loses her balance landing squarely on her butt.

The source of the light is Reena, a twenty-one year old female fairy. She is a mere three inches tall with wild red hair and shimmering wings clad in a plaid dress and tights. And, what is more she is Irish.

Reena quickly celebrates, thrilled with her new found freedom from the jar. She darts about the attic ecstatic paying no heed to Dorrie.

Dorrie watches a moment then rubs her eyes, opens them, and looks again. She is amazed. "What are you?" she asks her voice quaking a bit.

This is a puzzle to Reena. How could this adult-sized human not know what or who Reena is? Thoroughly insulted, she comes to a screeching stop in mid-flight, spins about, and zips across the room. She chooses to hover just inches from Dorrie's face.

"My name is Reena," the little fairy informs the woman of the house with a very heavy Irish brogue.

"Reena. What are you?" Dorrie asks again.

"Oh," a disgusted Reena crosses her arms in front of her chest and turns her back. Everyone knows who she is or at least she believed everyone knows. Don't they? Grams knew.

"Well?" Dorrie waits for an answer.

Reena spins around to face Dorrie. She sizes up the woman in her presence and concludes she does not approve of this stranger in her house, "And, who are you?"

"I'm Dorrie."

"Hm, Dorrie," Reena flits about a bit. "You know what I am."

"I do?" Dorrie asks.

Reena nods matter-of-factly.

Dorrie contemplates a few minutes. Her eyes suddenly light up in recognition. A fairy?"

Reena nods a bored acknowledgement. Her eyes drift to the open attic door. She glances over at Dorrie. The two make brief eye contact. Reena suddenly flies toward the doorway.

"Wait!" Dorrie yells.

Reena laughs at the thought of this woman telling her what to do. This little fairy has no intentions of wasting any of her valuable time in Dorrie's presence and flies out of the room at the speed of light.

Dorrie quickly jumps to her feet and chases out the door after the tiny fairy. "Hey, come back here!" she calls.

Reena is out of sight before Dorrie ever reaches the door. Knowing that the only direction she could have gone is downstairs, Dorrie races down to the landing.

She does not slow as she passes by the second floor. Her brisk pace continues until she reaches the base of the stairs on the main floor of the house. Dorrie stops abruptly and glances around. There is no Reena in sight.

Dorrie takes a moment to catch her breath. This gives her time to give the area a quick visual look over before she steps foot in the living room. She sees nothing. Nothing but things, inanimate objects, no fairy. "This is not going to be easy."

Dorrie walks past the large picture glass window. Its drapes are seldom drawn open anymore. The house has fallen into the state of gloom reflective of Dorrie's emotional condition.

"Where could something as small as that fairy hide?" she thinks and immediately corrects herself for having such a foolish thought. Dorrie knows all too well that there are hundreds of places in a house of this size that are more than a little bit capable of concealing her.

"Reena, come here. Come here, Reena," she calls as she slowly walks through the living room. "Reena?" There is only silence in response.

The bookshelf is the first place she searches. She pulls a few books out at a time to look behind them. Nothing.

The window's drapes rustle slightly. It goes unnoticed by Dorrie. She is on the other side of the room with her back turned to them.

Dorrie ponders the four overstuffed chairs in the room. She carefully tips each chair forward and looks. Due consideration was given that Reena could be hiding under one of them. Nothing. Next, she runs her hands along and under each cushion. Again, she finds no sign of the little fairy.

The sofa is the target on the search list. Dorrie reasons this must be where Reena is hiding. Not only because it is the only place left in the room that, so far, she has not yet searched but also because out of all the areas it is the only truly logical place any reasonable fairy would select.

All of this is Dorrie's opinion alone, of course. To her it does stand to reason as she believes it would for any reasonable and knowledgeable adult. After all, the sofa offers more than just a place of concealment; it also offers ready access and multiple escape routes its entire circumference.

Unbeknownst to Dorrie, she is close to Reena. At least she is in the same room. But, to her chagrin the fairy's location at this moment has nothing to do with the sofa.

Reena slipped into her hiding spot by accident mere seconds before Dorrie came thundering down the stairs. It was purely coincidental that she ended up here, behind the drapes. Just a fluke really. Reena just needed something fast and the window was the first place she past in her effort to flee the pursuing Dorrie.

Reena intends to stay behind the drapes as long as she deems necessary to avoid what she considers to be one very dreadful woman. Unfortunately, there is a price to pay for this choice location of concealment. To say that it is by far not the best location a fairy could have selected is an understatement. It is smothered in dust; the kind of dust which builds over a long period of time.

The little fairy accurately gathers that Dorrie must never or almost never opens the drapes. And, it is also quite obvious to her that the lady of the house has not taken them down for periodic cleaning in an equally long period of time. The build-up of dust speaks volumes of testimony to that fact. Dust covers the sill, the drapes, and now little Reena.

Reena's face wrinkles in disapproval. Try as she may she cannot avoid payment of the primary penalty, sneezing. "Ah, ah, ah choo!" Reena swallows her first of what shall soon become several sneezes.

It is not long after her extensive succession of sneezes begin that Reena decides she must never again use this area as a place of refuge. She shall, instead, preferably find one with cleaner air. After all, what her lungs inhale and the damage it can do to her is worth far more to her than the risk of a mere human such as Dorrie catching her.

Disappointment in not finding the illusive fairy hemmed by a lack of confidence causes Dorrie to begin to rethink her actions. Perhaps, she is being a tad bit more than foolish. Maybe, just maybe she is bordering delusional.

"This has got to be my imagination. Maybe I shouldn't have drunk that last glass of wine last night," Dorrie wipes her brow then eyes the sofa.

"No, this is crazy. A fairy," she laughs at herself and walks out of the living room.

No sooner does Dorrie leave the room than she turns on her heels and reenters. "Oh, what the heck. I have the time. Besides, who'd know?" she says glancing around making sure she truly is the only person in the room.

The jar shakes then vibrates violently across the attic floor. It comes to rest in an upright position. A few moments later it begins to glow.

George, a twenty year old, male fairy, who is just a mere two inches tall and quite stout for his height topples onto the floor in his top hat and tuxedo. He bounces across the floor several times, "Ouch, ouch, ouch. Rough landing, rough landing." All the while his hat stays in place. A remarkable feat as anyone who has ever worn one could attest to.

Dorrie busily searches under the sofa cushions. She has found nothing thus far so continues her quest to the floor area underneath. Frustration grips her at the realization that she cannot get a good visual by being on all fours. "Drat," she moans as she repositions herself. Whether she likes it or not, flat on her stomach provides her the best view.

George ricochets around the attic for a few moments trying to get not only his bearing but also seeking Reena. It is not long before he realizes Reena is nowhere in the attic. He pauses and contemplates on what he should do next.

"Where did you go?" he wonders to himself. "Ah," he follows the open attic door to the stairs. His stout form bounces off the walls like a soft marshmallow as he flies down the staircase to the home's main floor.

After he is clear of the stairs, George's momentum does not slow. He does not yet know where he is going to search for his friend. He is just going.

Somewhere in life someone had once told him that if you are not moving forward then you are moving backward. George is putting this into practice, literally. Luckily for him, though, Reena just happens to peek out from behind the drapes as he zooms by.

The little, female fairy's hand reaches out. She grabs him by the tuxedo's tails and pulls him behind the drapes the moment he comes within reach.

Whap! George's back hits the window. His eyes are wild and fill with fear. One flap of his wings and his eyes glaze over. Before Reena knows it, George becomes motionless against the window pane. He is in a catatonic-like state.

Reena shakes her head. George has always been predisposed to panic attacks. In all the years she has known him anything which is out of their version of norm sends him reeling.

"George, snap out of it. Snap out of it, George," Reena snaps her fingers in front of his face multiple times.

George is totally despondent.

Reena's face twists in aggravation. There is no time for this. Dorrie is on the prowl. Reena loses her patience and flies up and into George. She bumps him hard enough to snap him back into reality. Finally, there is a sign of movement. Even though it translates into a state of being startled, it is still better than no response at all.

"Huh?" he asks looking about with great anxiety. Sweat begins to pour profusely from his brow.

"We've got to hide," Reena grabs his hand and yanks him away from the window. "Come on."

They begin to fly toward the curtain leaving George's body imprint on the dusty window pane.

Reena suddenly stops, "No, wait."

George collides into her. "Oh, sorry," he says a bit embarrassed.

His words of apology are briefly acknowledged. There is far more important concern for the fairies at this moment, Dorrie. Reena is more intent on finding out if that awful Dorrie is still lurking in the area or worse yet, if she is just on the other side of the drapes.

She takes a quick peek through the drapes and feels immediate liberation and relief. Dorrie is nowhere in sight. Reena breathes a quick sigh of relief then grabs George's hand again and whoosh, up the stairs they go to the attic with George barely hanging on to his hat.

Dorrie, still lying on the floor in front of the sofa, softly calls, "Reena, come here. Come here, Reena." She stretches her arm as far as she can to reach even further under the sofa.

"Eugh!" Dorrie quickly withdraws her hand. She looks at it expecting to see something out of the ordinary like one would see in a horror flick. Whatever it was her hand made contact with cannot stay under the sofa. And, do not think that she has not thought about leaving it there. But, she knows she cannot.

So, Dorrie ever-so-bravely, in her opinion, reaches underneath the sofa again but this time determined to take firm hold of the unknown object. Does not matter what the thing is it does not belong on the floor under the furniture. She takes a deep breath then extends her arm as far as possible and finally lays hold of the object.

"Oh, those boys," Dorrie says as she extracts what she soon learns to be nothing more than one of her son's stale peanut butter sandwich.

Dorrie looks the sandwich over and then tosses it onto the coffee table. "The boys stopped eating peanut butter over a year ago," she says suddenly feeling disgusted with the state of their home.

Meanwhile upstairs, Devon and Daryl, the Sams' eight year old twin boys, have awakened and are getting dressed for school.

Their room, like the rest of the house, is in disarray. The twin beds are unmade, night stands are cluttered, sports paraphernalia is piled in a disorganized state in the corner, and toys surround the empty toy box. And, if that is not bad enough dirty clothes, dust bunnies, and dishes with crusted foods lie scattered under their beds.

"Hurry up," Devon tells Daryl. "You are such a slow poke," he says walking toward the door.

"I am not."

"You are too," Devon says firmly.

Daryl loosely ties his shoes and scrambles to catch up to his brother who is now stepping out of the room.

Reena is so preoccupied with fleeing the living room area before Dorrie can find them she inadvertently flies herself and George right past the boys' open bedroom door.

She does not as much as notice the pair standing in the doorway.

Devon freezes in his tracks when the two small blurs of light fly past at eye level. He shakes his head and rubs his eyes. "I need glasses."

"Huh?" Daryl asks.

"Nothing," Devon quickly realizes his brother has seen absolutely nothing. He in no wise is going to let on to his sibling that he saw a blur of light going down the hallway.

Devon is in no mood to stick around to see if that whatever it was comes back. He shoves Daryl toward the staircase, "Come on. The last one down has to do both of ours homework."

The boys rush out of their bedroom. They push and shove each other all the way down the stairs. Neither wants to lose to the other. It is a competition between them.

"I won," Devon proudly announces as he reaches the base of the stairs first.

"That's not fair. You always win," Daryl pouts.

"So? I always jump past the last step," he rubs Daryl's head as if to rub in the loss.

"It's not fair."

"Is too."

"Is not," Daryl whines.

The boys argue all the way into the kitchen. Neither of them notices their mother as they pass through the living room.

Dorrie is almost finished searching under the sofa when Dave enters the house. He was so distracted when he left for the college this morning that he forgot a very essential item to any professor, his briefcase. Fortunately, the briefcase is right where he left it, on the foyer's table.

Just as Dave reaches for it, Devon and Daryl race through the room towards the front door. A near collision occurs between father and sons.

"Don't run in the house," he reprimands the two.

"Yes, Dad," they acknowledge in unison.

"Where's your mom?"

Devon and Daryl do not hear him. They never slow their pace by as much as a little as they run out the door.

"Those boys," Dave mutters under his breath. He then turns his attention to finding his wife. "Dorrie, I'm home for a bit," he calls.

Dorrie, finally done with her search of the sofa is on her hands and knees. "Kind of early aren't you?"

Dave hears her but he does not see her. "Where are you?"

He starts to walk toward the kitchen when he catches a glimpse of Dorrie's hand waving to him from the other side of the sofa. "What are you doing down there?"

Dorrie grabs onto the sofa and begins to pull herself to her feet.

Dave steps up and extends a helping hand. "Lose something?"

"A fairy," she responds matter-of-factly.

At first, her words do not register. "What was that?" he asks her after a moment sure that he misunderstood her.

"A fairy," Dorrie dusts off her clothes.

Dave shakes his head. "A fairy."

"Yes," Dorrie steps away from the sofa.

Dave has known that his wife has been having greater difficulty coping with her grandmother's death than the rest of the family but, that is to be expected considering Grams had raised her. This, whatever it is that is currently going on with Dorrie he never could have imagined. Not in his wildest dreams did it ever occur to him that her grief would turn into such an extreme reaction.

"She's seeing things," he thinks to himself. "Perhaps she is just trying too hard to get back into a normal routine."

Concern fills his eyes and voice, "Hon, you're supposed to relax on your day off."

"I'm fine," Dorrie anxiously makes her way to the stairs.

Dave is close behind. He is on her heels every step of the way. "Seriously, what did you lose?" he tries to ask as nonchalantly as possible.

"I told you. A fairy," she slows just long enough to answer his question.

Two very upset fairies, Reena and George, float across the attic to the chest. George is more visibly troubled that their home was discovered than Reena. He glances at her off and on as they approach their jar.

"Who found our home?" he asks hovering just above it.

Reena stares down at the jar and slowly answers, "She said she lives here."

George shudders violently, "Oh, no, that means." He is choked up. A moment passes, "That means Grams is gone."

"George," Reena shakes her head in denial.

Dave reaches the stairs before Dorrie does and quickly blocks her path. He reaches out to her gently taking hold of her arms. "Let's talk, hon."

Dorrie is determined. This is not the time for talk. She has something very important to do. "Not now. The attic. You'll see," she shakes her head at him.

Dave's eyes follow Dorrie's as she looks up the staircase. "Okay," he concedes. "I'll go with you to take a look. But, it will have to be quick. I've got to get back to the campus soon."

Dorrie leads the way up the stairs. All Dave has done is slow her down. "Might as well go back to work right now because I don't know how long this is going to take," she thinks.

"George," Reena seeks his assistance.

George looks at the jar. Reena is leaning against it waiting for his help. He shakes his head thinking he knows what she wants.

"I'm not putting myself back in there," she says resolutely.

Reena brushes the bangs out of her eyes. Sometimes her stout friend could really get on her nerves. Like right now. "Stop assuming," she snaps back at him.

"Then what are you going to do?" George wants to know. "She'll be coming back you know."

"Which is why you need to stop your lip flapping and help me," she scolds. "We've got to get our home out of here."

George looks at the open doorway and then down at the floor. "I don't think you've fully thought through an exit plan. That woman is surely going to come back through that door. Unless, of course, you think that she may just choose to crash through the ceiling or rise up through the floor," he chuckles.

"Ooh, George, stow the humor. Out the window. We'll take it out the window and wait on the ledge."

That does sound like a more reasonable plan, "Okay." George descends halfway to Reena and comes to an abrupt halt. "Wait a minute. The ledge?" he looks over at the window. His eyes grow wide with fear. "Out, out as in outside the room?"

"Yes, George. As in outside the room."

"That is not a ground floor window."

Reena's eyes narrow. "That's right George. It's an attic window. You know the highest window in this house."

"But, I'm allergic to high places," he chuckles nervously. "You know what they say. The more firma the less terror."

Reena's eyes soften. "Sure, George, whatever you say. Of course you are. How rude of me not to remember," she says sweetly.

George nods and smiles. He finds it so comforting that she understands. This gives him false reassurance.

Deep down Reena could care less how George feels about heights or anything else for that matter. They need to temporarily relocate their home as quickly as possible. Those pounding footsteps on the stairs are not a product of her imagination. It is a very clear sign that some is coming.

"George! Now!" Reena's temper blows.

Shocked by her abrupt change, the stout little fairy scurries to assist. It is far a better fate for him to risk life and limb than face Reena's anger. Plummeting to his death off the ledge is a 'what if' scenario. Facing the damage Reena can do is a sure bet if he does not help.

"Well, since you put it that way," he excuses himself.

The primary lifting and shouldering the weight of the jar during transport rests mostly on Reena. George is merely keeping the jar balanced. And, that is a strain on his, for lack of a better word, muscles.

Once they are outside the window, the fairies set the jar on the ledge. Since the jar's circumference is bigger that the width of the ledge, the pair perch themselves on opposite sides of the jar to hold it steady.

The thought that neither of them knows how long they will have to wait here adds to George's already peaking stress level. Fear of heights, alone, has him almost paralyzed.

"At least the weather is nice today, George," Reena comments calmly surveying the few white clouds drifting across the blue sky.

George stares straight ahead unwilling to as much as move his lips in response. He is convinced that the least little thing might throw him off balance and send him plummeting over the ledge.

Dorrie is the first to enter the attic. Dave is close behind judging, in a professional sense of course, her every move, every word.

Dorrie confidently strides through the room oblivious to her husband's steady gaze. One sight of the jar will prove to her husband that she is not imagining things. In fact, she is so positive; she practically ran the stairs to get here.

"You'll see. It's right over here," she says rushing up to the cedar chest.

"Everything will be fine, hon," Dave slowly approaches her. He displays his concern for her well-being by placing his hand tenderly on her shoulder.

Dorrie does not notice. She is consumed with thoughts of the fairy and sloughs off his hand. "It's right there," she triumphantly points to the floor on the other side of the cedar chest.

"What?" Dave guardedly walks around the chest. He is not surprised by what he finds. There is nothing in front of the cedar chest but a stack of quilts. "I don't see anything here but quilts and a lot of dust," he informs his wife.

"What? No. That can't be," an alarmed Dorrie insists. "The jar it is right there." Dorrie goes to the front side of the chest.

Dave's brows furrow. He casts a sympathetic but doubtful look at Dorrie.

"It has to be here," Dorrie begins searching underneath the quilts.

"Hon, hon," Dave walks up to her. "There's nothing here but quilts."

Dorrie is in a mild state of shock. She leaves the quilts and begins searching the entire attic. "It was right here. Oh, that's right. I dropped it. Maybe it rolled..." Dorrie drifts off not finishing her sentence.

Dave is beginning to feel alarmed. His wife's mental state is more advanced than he thought. He thinks for a moment on the best angle from which to approach her. "Hon, no. It's all right. Really, it is."

Dorrie feels helpless. She knows what she saw but there is no reasonable explanation in her mind as to what could possibly have happened to the jar. And, worse yet, without the jar she cannot prove its existence to her husband.

Dave backs away. His heart hurts so for his suffering wife. Perhaps it will be better for him to take charge and get her the help she so desperately and obviously needs. His mind reels with a whole host of "what's next" scenarios. He shudders at the thoughts.

On the attic ledge, George's face is turning blue. He is starting into another panic attack. A painful, low groan erupts.

"Just a few more minutes, George," Reena whispers.

George does not respond.

"George," she whispers to him again.

"Yes?" George's voice is strained and his eyes are bulging.

"Just a few more minutes," she tells him.

"Okay," he responds barely audible.

In the clear skies overhead, a crow has ventured into new territory in hopes of garnering better eats. He dips and soars, his eyes painstakingly searching for some tasty morsel of food to take back to his mate.

The crow clicks his beak, "Something different, something like, like that!" He has spotted the fairies.

He just knew that if he dared to venture into this other neighborhood it could very well be a good scavenging session. Maybe it could be the best hunting expedition he has ever taken. Not fruitless like that last neighborhood he had flown to.

Circling overhead the crow realizes the little creatures are much smaller than what he usually takes back to the missus. Plus, these things are totally unknown to him. He stares at them trying to figure out what they could possibly be before finally deciding it does not matter. Technical labels have never affected his pallet.

"Perhaps, they will have a gourmet flavor to them," he licks his beak. "Mm, they just might be the most delectable morsels the missus has ever tasted."

The crow descends. He comes to perch on a branch of a large oak tree next to the Sams' house. From here, he can keep a watchful eye on his intended prey. In the meantime, a nice preening of his feathers is in order. "Must not gather food with dirty feathers," he smiles.

It is not long after the bird takes a seat on the branch than George notices him. "Reena," George stutters.

Reena is busy looking down on a beautiful flower bed next door. It is filled with some of her favorites; lilies, roses, chrysanthemums, irises, and gladiolas. She does not give George as much as a sideways glance, "Be quiet, George."

The crow clacks his beak. George begins to tremble violently. Still Reena has not noticed. It is not until the bird caws loudly disrupting her tranquility that Reena becomes alert to the pending danger.

Reena now feels a surge of panic but she takes care not to let it reflect in her voice so she can reassure George, "Soon, we will be able to get inside, soon."

The truth of the matter is Reena has not got one clue how soon the fairies will be able to reenter the attic. It is almost as if that Dorrie and the man with her are taking up permanent residency in there. In reality only a few minutes have passed since the fairies sought refuge out the window.

George does not hear a word Reena says. His eyes are fixated on the crow.

Devon and Daryl's earlier dash out of the house was short lived. Both boys soon realized they had missed breakfast and were hungry. Their stomachs are cranking on them so severely that they are making all sorts of gurgling noises.

So, Devon and Daryl make a conscious decision to return to the house and face whatever discipline their parents dished in their direction. Instead of finding themselves being confronted the moment they walk into the house, they are relieved to find their parents temporarily unavailable, distracted with something else.

"We lucked out this time," Devon tells Daryl.

"Yah."

It quickly dawns on the twins that if they hurry they could very well escape all parental encounter until much later in the day. And, since they are no different than the typical child, they know the later the better.   Because parents are generally too tired to give a child their full attention by the end of a busy day. And, where discipline is concerned from a child's perspective, that is a good thing.

The boys' quest for food leads them to take the most convenient items available for consumption. This morning it happens to be a filled cookie jar and a large, bottle of soda. Both items are sitting within their reach on the kitchen counter.

Devon is first through the kitchen door and immediately beads in on the cookie jar and soda. He grabs hold of them before Daryl can. Taking charge, putting himself first has always been part of Devon's character. It is almost as if his brother does not exist at times.

Daryl highly objects and resorts to his usual reaction, a tantrum. Now, depending on how Devon responds will have direct correlation to the severity of the tantrum. Daryl also has justification for his radical emotions. The cookies and soda were his idea. He had seen them first.

"Give me," his face is all puckered and turning red as he orders Devon.

"No," Devon quickly responds without a care as to the consequences.

"But, it was my idea," Daryl reminds him in a voice combining a scream and a whine.

"It was my idea," Devon argues. He intends to maintain control of the goodies and immediately cradles both under his arms. The degree of Daryl's actions does not matter to him at all.

Daryl's tantrum begins in earnest. A tear starts down his reddened cheek. He blubbers in a voice that is difficult to understand, "I want some, too."

"Me first," Devon is unyielding.

Daryl's face twists in determination. He growls as if he can scare his brother into giving him what he wants, which does not happen. So, next, he grabs for the cookie jar and bottle of soda.

Devon quickly turns his body away from Daryl trying to protect both from his brother's prying hands.

Daryl is insistent and resorts to pushing Devon off balance. He then seizes the opportunity to wrestle the item closest to him from his brother's control, the soda bottle.

Devon feels the bottle slipping out from under his arm and desperately tries to maintain control, "Let go!"

"No!" Daryl yells.

Devon is trapped between the counter and Daryl and is losing control of both the bottle and the cookie jar.

Dave and Dorrie can now vaguely hear the boys in the kitchen. They, too, are having a heated difference of opinion.

Dave steps toward the attic door. He is so preoccupied with Dorrie's state of mind that he almost steps fully down on the folded piece of paper on the floor. The vague sound of something crumpling underneath his shoe is heard. He stops and glances down to see what it could possibly be. "A piece of paper," he mumbles.

"What?" Dorrie asks indifferently.

Dave slowly moves his foot and picks up the paper.

Dorrie, still obsessed with searching the nooks and crannies of the room, catches a glimpse of his motions out of the corner of her eye. She takes time out of her search and approaches him to see what it is he has in his hand.

Dave shrugs nonchalantly. He hands it over to her without looking at it, "Just a piece of paper on the floor."

Dorrie takes the paper and immediately finds it is not just any piece of paper, it is a note. "I don't understand," she comments slowly unfolding it.

Dave shakes his head. He has absolutely no clue but an opinion is beginning to form.

Dorrie stares in amazement. The note is a handwritten message to her from Grams. "This is Gram's handwriting," she shares excitedly.

Dave cocks his brow, nods. His gesture has nothing to do with whether or not he believes her words. That nod is just a basic acknowledgement that he has heard her.

Dorrie's eyes begin to tear and her hands tremble. She reads the note out loud to him, "A special gift waits inside. You will find it in a mason jar. Treat with care and caution. Your gift is a cleaning fairy. Love, Grams."

Dave rolls his eyes. "Let me see that," he snatches the note from Dorrie's hand. He examines on both sides and then states, "Hon, I know how deeply you miss your grandmother. We all do. But, this is just too much. You really need to come to terms with her death."

"What?" Dorrie feels like someone just knocked the wind out of her. Dave's reaction to her grandmother's message totally stuns her.

"I'm sorry. I just can't do this. I miss her, too. It's a shame the boys really don't have any good memories of her but still, we both know that they are being affected by all of this as well," Dave steps toward the doorway.

Every ounce of Dorrie's body tenses. She is insulted and enraged. But, more importantly, she is hurt. "What? Ooh! How dare you!" she flies back at him.

Just as the parents are reaching a climatic point to their activity, the boys are quickly coming to theirs in the kitchen. Their fight for possession of the cookie jar and soda is nearing a close. Devon is losing his grip of not only the soda but the cookie jar as well.

"Stop!" Devon commands his brother feeling desperate.

Instead of heeding Devon's word, Daryl grabs the back of Devon's arm and pulls hard and fast. That does the trick. In the blink of an eye both the cookie jar and soda bottle plummet to the floor.

"Uh, oh," Daryl immediately steps back.

The boys' eyes are on the leaking soda bottle running into the broken cookies and remains of the jar. Both are speechless.

Dorrie has no intentions of letting go of the subject of her sanity any time soon. Dave's position that she is not thinking rationally and is therefore fabricating the fairy incident will be resolved.

When Dave had walked through the front door earlier he was hoping to pick up his briefcase, give his wife a quick hello, and return to work. Nice and simple. But, as things turned out that did not happen.

It is quite apparent that the couple still has those occasions when one spouse, usually Dave, will say something that will totally inflame the other, Dorrie. Once the words of offense are spoken a heated discussion ensues. And, it will last until a resolution Dorrie is willing to accept is reached.

Dave attributes difficulties in communication with Dorrie to genes. He is thoroughly convinced that she inherited one very hot temper from the Irish side of her family. It only stands to reason. After all, his British ancestors held the same belief.

Dorrie boldly places herself between Dave and the door before he can escape. "You think I miss Grams so much that I made this up?" she demands an answer.

"Well, hon, think about it. Logically, you know, from my perspective." Dave takes a step back. He hopes between his body language and his words to disengage from the whole conversation.

Dorrie will not allow that to happen. "Your perspective? Your perspective comes from years spent in books on psycho-babble," she lashes back.

Dave raises his hands to call a truce even if it is a temporary one.

"You don't believe me."

"Here," he hands the note back to Dorrie.

Dorrie waves the note in his face.

Dave shakes his head fully regretting having said anything questionable about a fairy's existence. "It doesn't matter what I believe. You're the one who claims to have seen a fairy."

His words do absolutely nothing to quell Dorrie's upset state. That will have to wait until a later time. Right now there is a temporary reprieve for him but it is only temporary. The couple's time out is called by the twins.

The boys have made enough noise between their yelling and dropping the cookie jar and soda bottle that they have not only been heard by their parents but also their neighbors.

"Devon and Daryl are in the kitchen from the sounds of it," Dave says feeling a sudden rush of relief. He now has a viable excuse to walk away bringing an end to their discussion for the time being. In this household the parents never put their discussions, heated or not, above their children.

Dorrie storms out the door with Dave on her heels.

"We'll finish this later," he says following her out of the room.

Reena and George have listened intently to Dorrie and Dave's argument. It was not that hard to do with the volume of their voices. The sudden peace in the attic comes as a blessed relief to the little fairies.

"About time," Reena exhales in frustration. When Grams was alive the house was always peaceful. There was no discord, no heated voices, and no hurtful words. Love reigned.

"Maybe they know we're here and they are just lying in wait for us to go back inside," George thinks out loud.

Reena dismisses that thought with a chuckle. "Sure. Then you can bloody well wait right here."

"I really think they killed each other," George adds.

Reena shakes her head at her friend. "Such drama George. They can't be lying in wait and dead," she shakes her head at him. "I think they left."

George considers the options, wait outside and possibly plummet to his death, wait outside and get snatched by the crow, or reenter the attic. It does not take long for him to come to the conclusion that being indoors is the preferable choice.

He tips his ear toward the window, listens a moment, and then agrees, "You are probably right. There was no blood-curdling scream, after all. You know, like there is in the movies."

Reena laughs at his logic. "Scotland Yard material, you aren't."

"Huh?" George does not get it.

"Never mind," Reena starts to stand.

"Reena," George calls her attention to a minor detail. Her movement has thrown the jar off-balance and it has begun to wobble unsteadily.

"Oh," Reena leans into the jar and stabilizes it.

Out of the corner of her eye she sees that George's eyes are bulging. "You okay?" she asks.

George, nervous, is speechless. The encroaching crow is all he can think about.

The movement of Reena brings the crow to reach the decision that it is time to make his move to snatch up the little treats. He hops along the tree branch getting closer by the second.

"Reena."

"What is this?" the crow is caught off-guard. He flaps his wings instinctively as the tree limb bends. It is too weak to support his weight. He will have to go airborne to get to the fairies.

"George."

George's teeth chatter severely. His entire body shakes, "I'm supposed to eat lunch, not be lunch."

Reena cannot argue with that. She does not intend to end her days in the belly of a bird.

"Reena," George says sharply.

Reena whips about and finds herself facing the crow. The bird has taken aim on her because she is the closest one to him.

"Come on, George. Let's take it back inside, now," she says none too soon.

Within the miniscule space of a blink of an eye, the fairies balance the jar between them and fly it through the window.

"They're getting away," panics the crow. He cannot get the speed he needs in time. For when he swoops down it is just as the window closes. Splat! The crow falls to the ground stunned and with a knot on his head.

This is one experience he has no intentions of repeating. The fairies quick maneuver has inadvertently ensured that it shall be a very long time before this crow returns to the neighborhood, if ever.

"Whew!" Reena wipes her brow. "That was too close."

George's face is flush. His blood pressure has soared. His breathing is rapid and shallow. His eyes bulge almost out of their sockets. And, then it happens. He passes out cold.

Reena finds herself suddenly trying to rescue the jar. She glances over at George to find he is not on the other side of it. Another quick look and she sees him drifting down to the floor, unconscious.

"Oh," she darts underneath the jar and balances it above her head. "George," she calls down to him.

George does not respond. His stout body makes impact. Fortunately, he lands in a thick layer of dust which cushions him.

Reena cannot deal with both George and the jar simultaneously. She must choose which one to put first. Since George is already on the floor and she cannot prevent him from making impact with it, she takes care of the jar.

Reena carefully floats the jar to the other side of the attic. There, she places it on the floor behind the dresser. It will be concealed and private for the fairies.

She then rushes over to George. He is fine and beginning to regain consciousness by the time she arrives at his location.

"George," she ever-so-lightly taps him on the cheeks.

He opens his eyes and looks around then touches his arms and legs and then he pats the floor around him. To his surprise he is still alive. There is no crow, no window ledge. He is in one piece, back in the attic.

"I'm alive!" he yells getting on his feet.

"You scared me. Don't do that ever again," Reena scolds.

George dusts himself off and adjusts his hat. "Rest assured, that was not planned."

Reena shows George where she placed their home.

George gazes down on the jar and asks, "Why there?"

"That layer of dirt here means they never come this far into the attic," Reena explains.

"I see," George smiles.

Both fairies venture down to the jar. They have feel they have had enough adventure for one day and are ready for a bit of a rest.

Devon and Daryl hear their parents' approaching footsteps. Neither of them wants to face their mom and dad. They scramble to flee the kitchen before they get caught. But, both are in such a hurry trying to make it to the back door that neither pays any attention to what the other one is doing.

The boys collide into each other multiple times before Devon takes charge. He grabs Daryl by the arm and pulls him out of the kitchen, "Come on."

Out the back door and across the lawn the twins flee just as Dave and Dorrie enter the kitchen. The boys run as if their tails are on fire.

"What a mess!" Dave exclaims entering the kitchen.

"Oh, my," Dorrie is aghast. "Right in the middle of the floor," she says stepping over the shattered cookie jar and soda puddle.

Dorrie opens a closet door and gets out a mop and broom. The floor has soda footprints leading to the back door. "Better get this cleaned up before it has a chance to set or get stepped in any further than it already has been."

"Those boys need a good..."

Dorrie quickly interrupts him, "You're the one who said train them with a soft hand." She starts to sweep up the broken pieces.

"Yeah, don't remind me," Dave storms up to the back door and opens it.

"Dave," Dorrie tries to avert his attention.

The boys finally come to a stop to catch their breath. They have reached the shrubs edging their yard at its furthermost point.

"What now?" Daryl asks.

"In here," Devon crawls between the shrubs on his hands and knees.

Daryl follows.

Dave looks out the door and calls, "Devon, Daryl!"

There is no sight of the boys.

"They've headed for the hills till the coast in clear," Dave turns away from the door. "I'll have to deal with this later. I've got to get back to the college. Been gone too long already."

"But, Dave."

Dave steps past Dorrie on his way out of the kitchen. He pauses on the opposite side of the room, "Tell them they're grounded. When you see them. Which probably won't be for awhile."

Dorrie nods, "Sure."

The boys, hiding behind a bush, spy the car as Dave backs it out of the driveway.

"Dad looks mad," Daryl observes.

"It's your fault."

"My fault?" Daryl shrieks.

"If you hadn't grabbed my arm…"

The boys begin pushing and shoving each other.

Dorrie steps out the front door. She hears the boys' commotion then catches a glimpse of Devon's head on the other side of her car. This is used to her advantage.

Quietly she closes the door. She then hurries through the house to the back door and exits. A few moments later she walks up on her sons, "Devon, Daryl."

Stunned, the boys freeze in their tracks.

"How'd she sneak up on us like that?" Daryl asks Devon.

Devon does not respond. He is still in a state of shock. The boy has always known his mother had eyes in the back of her head but this? This is guerrilla tactics, a stealth maneuver, something moms are not supposed to be able to do.

"Can't you two behave for just a little while?" Dorrie breaks the silence with an aggravated voice.

Devon and Daryl shrug, "Yes, Mom."

Dorrie points to the front door, "Get ready for school. Now."

Devon and Daryl run into the house. The door slams shut behind them.

Dorrie enters to find them pushing and shoving each other up the staircase to their room. She shakes her head. "This is going to be a long day," she mutters to herself.

"See what you did," Devon blames Daryl.

"You did it."

Devon shoves Daryl into the bedroom, "No, I didn't. You did."

Daryl jumps off the bed, "Uh, uh. Did not."

"Did too."

***

The fairies little home is comfortably nestled on the floor behind the dresser. Reena does not approve of the area one-hundred percent but it does offer an element which is much needed; that of privacy.

"This will be a private place where we need not fear discovery," she tells George with confidence.

George agrees.

Unfortunately, though, this hideaway has come with a price. It is very, very dusty. Reena figures they can tolerate it for awhile until she gets around to cleaning it herself. But, that can wait. Both fairies are tired from this day's activities.

The two small shadows of the fairies reflect off the jar's dim light as they settle into their beds. A good night's sleep is all Reena desires.

"Good night, Reena."

"Good night, George," Reena barely gets the words past her lips before she drifts into slumber.

The jar's light goes out.

Dorrie is boiling on the inside. The whole issue with Dave has festered deep inside of her all day. Everything he had said to her in the attic kept going through her mind like a broken record. Now, that they are alone she can start venting her thoughts, letting him know exactly how she feels. And, the beauty of it all is she can do it without saying so much as one word to him.

A handful of utensils clatter out of Dorrie's hand into the dishwasher. Her foot comes up and shuts the washer's door.

Dave is over at the table picking up the dirty plates and utensils. He has been taking thoughtful glances at Dorrie trying to judge her temperament. That is, until the dishwasher door slammed shut.

All through dinner ideas of how to smooth things over with her passed through his mind. He realizes he is at such a loss. This is the first time in their marriage that his entire educational prowess serves no useful benefit.

Dave picks up the last of the dishes and slowly approaches the sink. So far so good. He steps forward and gently paces the dishes down in front of Dorrie.

Dorrie watches him out of her peripheral vision paying him absolutely no heed. She is doing what a woman can do best; choosing not to communicate when he so desperately wants to. Inside she smiles knowing that her silence will eat at him.

Dave, who came from a household of sisters, knows the silent treatment ploy all too well. As with anything, though, a person can only take so much and he is already at the end of his rope. He cannot stand another moment of things not being right between them. So, he takes a risk.

Dave makes a conscious choice to begin with an explanation for his actions from earlier in the day, "Hon, about earlier. I know you loved your Grandmother a great deal. We all did."

Dorrie drops a plate in the dishwasher with a clatter.

"Hon," Dave persists.

"Don't talk to me," she tells him curtly without as much as a look in his direction.

"I'm just trying to tell you that denial..."

That word, denial, ricochets through Dorrie's head mercilessly. She abruptly interrupts him by sharply turning to face him. A plate is balanced on the fingertips of her right hand. Her eyes are narrow and intent.

For a moment, Dave is silent. But, unfortunately, his mute state only lasts the space of a few breaths. He is a little too persistent and his timing is all wrong.

"Denial is a natural step in the mourning process," he says with a sudden and glorious feeling of relief.

Dorrie spills. Her husband is so insensitive that he has repeated his mistake. She cannot ignore this. "Drop the subject. I'm not making this up. I do miss Grams something horrible at times but I know the difference between reality and imagination."

Dave listens intently thankful that she is finally opening up, telling him exactly what has been bothering her all evening. He is just not keen enough to know when to leave an issue alone.

"Hon, I'm just saying," he tries to again to explain.

"Shut up," Dorrie orders. She is leaving no room for doubt that this is not a subject that can be easily swept under a rug. And, even more importantly, she refuses to discuss any part of it with him any time in the near future.

He is again perplexed. His words are not working. The apology he had mentally rehearsed all day was fumbled the moment he opened his mouth. He wants so desperately to relate to her but is stumped on how to accomplish it.

Dave returns to the table, picks up the bottle of wine, and sets it on the counter. He watches Dorrie as he walks up to her again. Perhaps, a tender touch will get his point across. All he really wants her to know is that he loves her no matter how confused or ill she is right now. Surely, she will be able to see that. So, he reaches his hand and gently touches her shoulder.

The moment Dave's hand makes contact with Dorrie, her temper flares. She sharply pushes him back and quickly grabs for the broom which has been propped against the cabinets nearby.

Dave stares in disbelief at Dorrie's reaction. It is not until the bristles of the broom are mere inches away from making impact with him that he comprehends she really intends to hit him.

"I saw a fairy," she spells the letters to the word out for him. "Fairy, period. No discussion, end subject," she says resolutely.

Dave takes her by surprise deftly catching the bristles of the broom then jerking it away from her.

"Hon," he makes eye contact with her.

Dorrie's typically soft brown eyes are filled with anger.

"On second thought," he thinks perhaps retreat would be wisest. "Okay, hon," he tells her. "Whatever you say."

Oh, now he has really done it. The word whatever totally infuriates her. He knows full well how much she loathes that word, especially during times of discord. "Whatever I say?" she explodes. Another plate is sent hurling in Dave's direction.

He ducks. The plate sails across the kitchen splattering food particles on the cupboards and floors before it crashes against the wall. Shattered bits of it scatter across the floor.

"You think I wrote that note. That Grams died and now I'm off my rocker," she screams.

In the attic, the mason jar shakes. Its glow increases in intensity from faint to brilliant. An irritated Reena mumbles under her breath. She had been sleeping so peacefully, so snuggly in her cotton ball bed.

Reena jumps off her bed. She paces around, stepping over small piles of raisin pieces, bread crumbs, sunflower seeds, and jerky that are scattered throughout their home. Covering her ears brings no relief. The yelling Dorrie can still be heard.

Reena kicks at the floor. Her foot sends up a plume of golden fairy dust. The dust drifts across to George's bed and covers his face.

George wakes, coughs, and wipes the dust off his face. "Reena?" he asks still half asleep.

There is no response from the female fairy. She is spinning upward, oblivious to everything but the feuding couple downstairs.

The lid pops off the jar and clatters to the floor.

"Reena?" George sits up, rubs his eyes.

Reena is a blur as she flies out of the jar.

"Where are you going?" he asks in mid-yawn.

Reena does not hear him. She is on a mission, flying at light speed out of the attic. The sooner the couple quiet down the sooner she can get back to sleep. Judging from the duration of the dispute they are having it is obvious to her that they need a fairy visit, an upset fairy visit.

Dave and Dorrie are still entrenched in their heated communication when Reena flies into the room unnoticed. To her horror, the floor is littered with pieces of several broken dishes.

Dave backs almost to the other side of the room to get further away from Dorrie. Every time his foot steps down more plate pieces are crushed beneath his shoes.

A plate crashes in front of Dave. "How dare you!" Dorrie yells.

"Dorrie, hon, I was only trying to say there are better ways to ask for help." Dave has quickly begun to realize that he is very much backed into a corner and there will be no easy way out of this tirade Dorrie is throwing.

Dorrie reaches for the last plate.

Dave raises his hands in surrender. "I'm sorry."

Dorrie firmly grasps the plate. She mocks him as she brings it to chest level, "Sorry?"

Reena hovers nearby, hands on hips, and determined. "Enough already!" she yells.

Dave and Dorrie freeze in their tracks. The two look at each other then cautiously eye the kitchen. Without moving as much as one small muscle Dave meekly asks, "Who said that?"

Dorrie's eyes widen and then a very smug look washes across her face.

Reena flies into Dave's face. "I said that. Be quiet. It's past my bedtime."

"Told you!" Dorrie hurls the plate at Dave.

The plate hits Dave square in the chest. "Ouch! I didn't even see that one coming."

"Ha! Serves you right," Dorrie gloats.

Reena flies up to Dorrie.

George, who has followed Reena to the kitchen, peeks in from the doorway.

Dave stands quietly wondering if he, too, is having hallucinations now.

Reena buzzes around Dorrie like a pesky fly. Dorrie bats at her to no avail.

"Oh, this is not good," George shudders.

Devon and Daryl toss in their beds. They finally moan, roll over, and face each other.

Devon covers his head with his pillow and moans. A moment later he tosses the pillow across the room hitting the closet door.

"Why does Mom always break dishes when she and Dad fight," Daryl asks.

Devon sits up in his bed, "I think it's a rule for married people." He then gets out of bed and closes their bedroom door.

Downstairs in the kitchen, Reena screams at full volume at Dorrie, "Stop it! Stop it! Stop it!"

"Oh, my, oh, my," George wrings his hands.

Dorrie's hands bat again at Reena barely missing the tiny fairy.

That only exacerbates Reena. She grabs handfuls of Dorrie's hair and yanks with all her might.

Dorrie shrieks from the pain. Her hands automatically go to the top of her head in defense.

"Stop it!" Reena yells again.

Dorrie quickly gets still. She takes a deep, slow breath and concedes, "All right."

Reena waits a moment and then very slowly lets loose of Dorrie's hair. She then turns around to leave the room and finds Dave smirking at her. "You think I'm funny?"

Dave makes the mistake of laughing out loud. What seems like a nanosecond later, a very furious red-headed blur confronts him. He scoffs in response.

Reena's fists come up. She makes boxing motions at Dave, "Come on, come on tough guy."

Dave laughs again.

Reena bops him on the end of his nose hard enough to leave a welt.

"Ouch, that hurt," he rubs his nose.

Reena points and laughs then races out of the kitchen with George flying as her wingman.

"Oh, Reena, I wish you hadn't done that. I really wish you hadn't done that," George says nervously.

Reena makes mockery of George's concern.

Dorrie and Dave are left alone in the kitchen. They stare at each other in silence for several minutes.

Dave breaks the barrier, "You said there was a fairy, as in one. I think I saw two."

"Her fist carry such a blow that you're left seeing double?" Dorrie smirks.

"Ha, funny," Dave exhales. "That little thing carries a punch."

"Right, sure."

The mason jar glows softly welcoming Reena and George home. They enter.

Up off the floor the lid rises to the top of the jar. It floats down onto the opening and spins closed.

Both fairies snuggle down into their beds satisfied that they shall have a peaceful slumber now.

"Okay, now what Mr. Psychologist?" Dorrie asks Dave.

Dave shakes his head. "Wait and see?"

Disgusted, Dorrie slams out of the kitchen.

The darkened jar begins to glow. Inside, George sits on his cotton ball rubbing his stomach.

"Reena, Reena, you awake?"

Reena's eyes pop open. She had just drifted into a deep sleep. "Go to sleep, George." Her eyes close.

George twiddles his thumbs. "I've been thinking," he continues. "You awake?"

Reena rolls over to face him. There will not be any sleeping until George finishes whatever it is he feels he needs to say.

"Yes, George, you've been thinking."

"We missed dinner."

Reena moans, "It's too late for dinner."

"A little midnight snack to tide me till breakfast?" he coaxes.

Okay, she stands corrected. There will not be any sleep until George's stomach is satisfied. She knows from decades of experience that George will only continue his whining until he gets food into his stomach. Reena pours herself out of bed, "Okay."

Dave snores soundly in the couple's bed unlike his wife. Dorrie lies perfectly still on her back. She stares up at the ceiling without blinking. This has been a very miserable day followed by an even worse evening for her.

Throughout the entire day, her husband had not even the most minor thread of decency to consider that perhaps he was wrong, that his assumption regarding her emotional state was ill-founded. It was not until he got bopped on the end of his nose that he even considered for one second that she was telling him the facts. And, then what was his reaction? Wait and see.

"You are the most infuriating person sometimes," she rolls over taking the covers with her. Her eyes immediately close in the hopes of falling into a deep amnesiac slumber.

Dave continues to snore undisturbed. He has grown use to her taking ownership of the covers over the years.

George leads the way to the kitchen like a point man on an expedition. He smacks his lips repeatedly in eager anticipation of what goodies may lie ahead in the kitchen as they go.

"It wouldn't hurt for you to skip a meal once in awhile," Reena yawns.

George's pace slows. He looks down at his stomach and rubs it, "Mm. I guess."

"Like when I'm sleeping."

Once they are in the kitchen, Reena cannot believe her eyes. That woman Dorrie has gone off and left smashed plates everywhere on the floor. And, oh, the food splatters are just as atrocious. "How could she treat Gram's house this way?"

George pays no heed to the mess. He is not much of one for details especially those regarding cleanliness. The fruit bowl, on the other hand, catches his interest right off the bat. It is more fitting to his area of expertise.

He flies straight over to the bowl and makes himself comfortable on top of a cluster of grapes. His mouth waters as he eyes them. "Mm," he pokes at the first.

"Too hard," George says. He pokes at a second grape. "Too soft," he determines. The third one is a winner. One poke, "Just right."

George plucks the plucks the plump fruit. He takes a bite to find it is particularly sweet and juicy. "Mm, good, very good."

Reena shakes her head. Not at George but at the kitchen as a whole. Not only are there smashed remnants of plates everywhere she looks but the sink is full of dirty pots and glasses plus the counter tops are wretchedly filthy. And, then there is the floor. Bad enough shattered plates cover a good portion of it but it is also filthy from general foot traffic.

"George," she sighs.

Her companion is contentedly munching on the grape. He chooses to tune out anything that does not smell or taste like food.

"George," Reena repeats herself at a volume he cannot continue to ignore.

"Yes?" he nonchalantly responds still focused on the grape.

"Look at this," Reena waves her hand indicating the state of the kitchen.

George lazily floats off the bowl. Of course he takes his grape with him. He continues to munch as he floats upward. Once he has gained altitude he is in a good position to see exactly what it is that Reena in clamoring about.

"Oh, that," he says nonchalantly as if it were an after thought.

"What?" Reena cannot believe that George, in spite of his personal habits, could ignore this.

"Messy people," George adds before casually returning to the fruit bowl.

Reena scowls at him. Bad enough she was awakened from a sound sleep twice in one night but to expect her to tolerate this sty? That will not happen.

"Hold on," she says in a very firm voice.

"Ah, Reena, we just got here," George protests. But, he knows that nothing he can say will deter her from making an area clean once her mind is set.

"Can't stand this mess," she mutters under her breath.

George exhales then begrudgingly sets his prized grape down. He needs both arms free to embrace the banana in preparation for what is coming next.

Reena begins to spin, slowly at first then gradually increasing in speed.

"Won't even let a fairy finish his meal first," George complains.

Broken plates come off the floor and land in the trash can. The dishwasher door opens. George's half-eaten grape flies up off the counter and lands in the trash with a horrified George looking on.

"Oh, boulder dash," he exclaims holding tightly onto the banana.

George is next to feel the effects caused by the turbulent air movement created by Reena's spinning. His body lifts off the banana and is suspended in the air. He tightens his grip on the fruit feeling it squish underneath its skin.

Dirty dishes rise up out of the sink and enter the dishwasher. The dishwasher door shuts.

George's hat drifts off his head. He quickly grabs it and tucks the brim between his teeth then wraps his arm back around the banana.

Reena levitates the wine bottle staring at its label in fascination while a sponge wipes the counters down. She comes to a sudden stop. Her eyes cannot believe the picture on the label. It is one of grapes.

"Gram's juice," she squeals.

George's body lands on the banana with a thud. Banana immediately oozes through the peel and covers the front of his clothes. "Reena?"

"Okay, George."

George crawls off the fruit.

Reena perches herself on top of the wine bottle.

A drawer opens and a straw floats out and across the kitchen.

Reena plants her feet on the lip of the bottle and pulls on the cork with both hands. The bottle's cork pops off.

"What are you doing?" George asks as he wipes banana off his clothes. He has never having seen her do anything like this before.

The cork, with Reena attached, shoots across the kitchen. "Gram's juice," is all the response she gives.

George, distracted for a moment, looks at the floor. "I say, Reena," he points. "You missed a spot."

Reena lets go of the cork. She nods acknowledgement but any further cleaning will just have to wait. In her opinion there is far more important business at hand; wine.

"In a minute," she grabs the straw in mid-air.

"But, Grams said that juice wasn't for us." George walks around surveying the remaining grapes.

"Hush. Grams isn't here," Reena inserts the straw into the wine bottle and proceeds to take big gulps of wine.

"But, Reena."

She glares at George, takes a few more swallows, and smacks her lips.

"Okay," she hiccups. "You are going to help."

A mop and bucket come out of the closet.

Reena burps and hiccups simultaneously.

The mop goes into the bucket and wrings itself out.

"George, take the trash out," she says between hiccups.

Reena takes a few more sips of wine emptying the bottle. She then tosses it in the trash can.

George lazily rises into the air. "Why do I always have to be the one to take out the trash? Just do that wavy thing and make it take itself out."

Reena ignores George. She perches herself on the end of the mop handle. The hiccups continue while she dances the mop across the floor.

George zips past her to the trash can spinning Reena like a top.

Reena topples into the trash can. The can falls over onto its side spilling its contents onto the freshly mopped floor. Reena's hair falls about her face.

"George!"

George turns to find Reena and the trash strewn on the floor. He looks at her a thoughtful moment, removes his hat, and then scratches the top of his head, "Why'd you do that?"

Reena glares at him.

"Oh, kay," George puts his hat back on. "Guess I don't need the answer to that question. You don't need to get all huffy about it."

Upstairs, Daryl cannot sleep. He is still hungry. Several hours of trying to go to sleep have only left him wide awake with his stomach still grinding on him.

"Devon," he whispers his brother's name testing to see if he is awake. There is no response.

Daryl waits a few moments then slips out of the bedroom. He quietly makes his way down the stairs and through the house. At the kitchen door he stops. He makes a quick check over his shoulder to make sure he is alone before he enters. So far, so good. He smiles.

Reena's acute hearing picks up on the sound of approaching footsteps. She wastes no time whisking the mop and bucket back into the closet.

"Someone is coming," she warns George.

"Huh?" Startled, George instantly panics and flies himself smack into a cupboard door. He is knocked to the floor unconscious.

"Oh, George," Reena straightaway flies to the sink and retrieves a drop of water from the faucet. She carries it over to her friend not noticing Daryl's entry into the kitchen.

George coughs to consciousness with one splash of water. His eyes open just in time to see Daryl standing over them.

"Hey," Daryl says excitedly.

Reena slowly looks up. At first she sees a pant leg. She continues to look upward until she sees Daryl smiling down on them.

"Oh," Reena gasps. She grabs George's hand and pulls him to the top of the refrigerator.

"Come back here," Daryl chases after them.

Devon enters the kitchen unexpectedly. He woke up the moment Daryl had opened their bedroom door.

"What are you doing?" Devon asks.

"I saw them," Daryl points at the top of the refrigerator.

Devon cocks his head, suspiciously eyes his brother then the refrigerator, "Them?"

"Uh, huh," Daryl says emphatically.

"Let's see," Devon seriously doubts his brother. There is only one way to find out, though, and that is to look for himself.

Daryl gets a dining room chair and positions it in front of the refrigerator. "Up here?" he asks climbing onto the chair.

"Yes."

Reena and George huddle together behind the artificial plant. George is trembling so violently that Reena's body is shaking too.

Devon peeks over the top of the refrigerator. At first, he sees nothing but dust and the artificial plant.

"Nothing here," he tells a disappointed Daryl.

"Now," Reena whispers to George. Both fairies suddenly dart out from behind the plant. They continue flying at light speed until they are clear of the kitchen and those boys.

A startled Devon falls off the chair with a clamor landing on his butt.

"There they go," Daryl screams excitedly.

Devon pushes the chair out of the way with his feet.

"You okay?" Daryl asks helping Devon stand.

Devon rubs his butt, "That hurt."

The boys run out of the kitchen.

Dorrie turns on the bedroom light. An awful noise has awakened her. "Oh, if I have to get out of this bed," she thinks to herself. "You'll wish I hadn't."

"Boys! Get back in bed," she calls down to Daryl and Devon.

"Just getting a drink, Mom. We're coming," Devon calls back.

The boys slowly walk up the stairs keeping a watchful eye out for flying fairies as they go.

"Where'd they go?" Daryl wonders.

Devon shakes his head, "I don't know."

Dorrie calls again, "I'm waiting."

The boys acknowledge her in unison, "Yes, Mom. We're coming."

"We gotta go to bed," Devon says.

Daryl moans. Sleep is not what he wants to do right now. Exploring the house for fairies seems like a much better idea.

***

The following morning a very haggard looking Dave sits at the kitchen counter. His throbbing head is propped on his left hand. The other hand holds his morning cup of coffee. He takes a few drinks, sets it down, and then eats a dry piece of toast. It is just enough to tide him until lunch.

Dorrie slowly walks through the kitchen still yawning from lack of sleep. Her hair is in disarray and there are noticeable bags under her eyes. She almost has to drag herself to the refrigerator to start the morning kitchen routine.

"You look a little rough this morning," Dave comments under his breath. He is not yet awake enough to think through his words and their possible repercussions before he speaks to her.

Dorrie waves him off still feeling numb from yesterday. He is quite lucky that she is so tired his words do not register. Otherwise, this day would be starting off with yet another one of their very heated discussions.

She yawns wide as she pulls sandwich fixings from the refrigerator and places them on the counter. Reaching for the bread, she suddenly stops. Something is different. Something about this room is very different.

Dorrie eyes the counter then the floor. She turns and checks the sink. The trash can is empty. There is no sign of broken dishes and the sink is empty. All the dirty pots are in the dishwasher.

"Oh, honey," she assumes he cleaned the kitchen as a form of an apology. "How sweet," she smiles at her very thoughtful husband.

"Huh?" Dave responds not having a clue as to what she is referring to.

Dorrie indicates the kitchen with a sweeping motion of her hand. "So sweet." She leans across the counter and kisses him on the cheek.

Dave is thoroughly confused, "I don't know what you're talking about."

Dorrie chuckles, "Cleaning the kitchen for me?"

Dave laughs at her sense of humor, "Me? Come on, honey. All I did was clean up the trash can. Boys must have knocked it over last night. Oh, and I put the dining room chair back."

Dorrie is surprised, "Say what? You didn't do the dishes and?"

Dave shakes his head.

Dorrie and Dave make eye contact. "Well, if you didn't do this, who did?" Dorrie asks.

"Don't know but whoever it is we should hire them."

A glimmer appears in Dorrie's eyes.

"No," Dave quickly asserts. "There's no such thing as fairies. They are myth. Made up. Pretend. Created out of imagination."

"Gram's note said."

Dave shakes his head discounting the thought.

"We saw her last night. Can't deny that," Dorrie points her finger in Dave's face.

Suddenly uncomfortable, Dave rises from his seat. "We think we saw her last night," he says. "We'll talk later. I've got to get to work."

"But, Dave," Dorrie wants, no needs his affirmation before he walks out the door.

Dave grabs his briefcase off the counter. "I'll see you tonight." A moment later he is out the door and gone before the subject of anything fairy can be brought up.

Dorrie frowns, "Oh, Dave." She looks around irritated. A moment later she sloppily creates two sandwiches. She places them in the lunch sacks and sets them to the side.

Devon and Daryl run into the kitchen pushing and shoving each other.

"What now?" Dorrie asks sharply.

Devon and Daryl stop a moment and look at their mother then at each other.

"Daryl is wearing my shirt and won't take it off," Devon pushes Daryl.

"Stop," Dorrie orders.

The boys call a truce as they continue through the kitchen.

"All right. What kind of cereal do you want for breakfast?"

Devon and Daryl whisper amongst themselves. They had reached a previous agreement to ditch school so that they could "fairy hunt". Problem is, neither of them had thought the whole thing through or one of them would have realized their mother is always in the kitchen at this hour of the morning. Now they have to punt.

"Well?" Dorrie asks.

The boys exchange brief looks.

"Nothing," Daryl answers.

"Nothing? You've got to eat something," she insists.

"Can't. We're late," Devon explains.

"Oh." Dorrie looks at the wall clock. "It's not quite seven in the morning, and, you're late?"

Devon and Daryl grab their lunch sacks.

"Gonna play basketball before school," Devon explains.

"You guys don't even like basketball," Dorrie counters.

"Do now," Devon and Daryl race out the door.

"I see."

The moment the twins are out of sight they give each other high fives.

"Way to go!" Devon congratulates the both of them.

Dorrie looks at the door a moment, then at the wall clock. She shakes her head. "Girls would have been so much easier."

A whisper of the sun's rays filter across the attic's floor. Everything is peaceful and quiet. Nothing stirs. The door to the attic opens. Its lone ceiling fixture light comes on. Dorrie enters.

Dorrie's quest this morning has nothing to do with a fairy. Instead, she is here because the memories of her grandmother have brought her.

Dorrie is on a quest to settle her spirit. Dealing with Grams' death has been so difficult for her. Yet, she knows that she must get through the mourning process if life is to ever return to a state of normalcy for her family.

The attic may hold the key Dorrie needs in order to come to terms with Grams' passing. It is here, in the attic that her memories of Grams are the strongest.

Perhaps it is because only she and Grams ever came in here when she was alive. Or, maybe it is because Grams' personal effects are stored here. Then again, it just may very well be because this was where Dorrie spent most of her childhood playing with Grams looking on. Deep down Dorrie knows it is more likely a combination of all these things.

Dorrie picks up the quilts and dusts them off. She feels horrible for having treated them so carelessly yesterday. Each one is carefully placed back in the cedar chest and the lid is quietly closed. A tear trickles down her cheek.

As a toddler, she spent many long hours playing in this chest. It was her pirate's ship and she, the captain. A broken pocket watch was just one of the many treasures her ship held.

Dorrie shakes herself. She cannot deal with this right now, not so early in the morning. The fairy comes to her mind. Where did it come from? How did it get in the cedar chest? Did the fairy belong to Grams? If it did, how long did she have it? Was the fairy a secret Grams held within her for years? And, finally, if Grams had a fairy, why did she not tell Dorrie?

"Reena," she whispers. The little fairy surely has the answers to her many questions. All she has to do is find her.

The attic is so quiet. Only the sound of Dorrie's footsteps are heard. Dorrie walks toward the window. She stops and looks at the furniture pad in the corner.

"No," she shakes her head. Her eyes come to rest on the dresser. "Reena?" she calls approaching it.

"Reena?" Dorrie stops in front of the chest of drawers. She calls again, "Reena?"

The jar vibrates a little at first and then shakes violently before it becomes still. Inside their home, Reena jumps to her feet. She brushes the bangs away from her eyes.

"Oh," she moans and stomps her feet. "What?"

George, who is soundly sleeping in a fetal position, snorts and smacks his lips. He totally unaware of the disturbance.

Reena is highly irritated at being awakened from her sound slumber, especially by that woman. A wicked little smile crosses her face. "No sense in experiencing this alone," she tells herself.

A moment later, Reena takes hold of George's bed and yanks. "My sleep shant be the only one disturbed."

Poor sleeping George is sent rolling onto the floor with a thud. "Ah, Reena," he complains. But, a few seconds later he is asleep again. George quickly falls back into slumber the moment he leans against his ever so soft bed.

Reena is enraged. She paces back and forth at her wits end. "As if it's not bad enough listening to you snore all night. Oh, no, now I have to listen to that woman scream my name," she her hands are formed into fists at her side.

George is fully awake now. No one, not even he, can sleep through a Reena tirade. Her voice could pierce the furthest most reaches of the galaxy. "I don't hear anyone screaming but you," he yawns.

What George does or does not hear makes absolutely no difference to Reena. It is what her poor ears have heard that counts. And, she knows beyond a shadow of a doubt that woman will not cease until she has to.

Dorrie is still looking through the drawers of the dresser. She carefully and slowly opens and closes each one having started with the bottom drawer. Each drawer is given a thorough inspection. But, to her disappointment, they are all empty. There is no sign of the fairy.

"Back to reality," she mumbles under her breath. A moment later, when she turns to leave the attic, she is not only suddenly but, pleasantly startled. There, before her very eyes is a fairy, Reena to be exact.

"What?" a heated Reena demands.

Words twist between Dorrie's vocal chords and her lips and come out as stuttering, "You are real."

Reena exhales in disgust. Was this all this woman wanted was to tell her she is real? Reena's eyes narrow. She cocks her head. "Go away," she tells Dorrie.

Dorrie silently shakes her head. She does not want to go away. There are too many questions to be answered. Plus, there is one husband who really does not believe as yet. Going away? This is her house. She will be going no where.

Reena glares at Dorrie unrelentingly. A long moment passes between the two as they size each other up.

The silence is broken by Reena when she asks in a demonstrative tone, "What do you want?"

"The first break through in communication," Dorrie thinks to herself without a clue as to where to start the conversation. And, the fact that she is flustered does not help her a bit.

Dorrie can barely form a cohesive sentence. After all she is the one who is supposed to ask the questions, not be put on the spot by a fairy. She continues to stutter, "Well, well, well I, well I just thought…"

"Don't think. Go away," Reena rudely cuts Dorrie off with her command.

Dorrie hesitantly turns and looks at the door a very long moment before looking back at Reena, "But, I…"

Reena's face flushes a deep red. Her face twists hard from irritation and her little body trembles all over. "Now!" she yells.

"But," Dorrie is confused. She found the fairy or the fairy found her. She is not quite sure which but regardless of who did what they are finally face to face. Now would be the perfect time to talk or so she thought. Evidently she is most incorrect.

Reena becomes a blur as she flies in a zigzag pattern in front of Dorrie.

Try as hard as she might, Dorrie's eyes cannot keep track of her movements.

Reena comes to a stop just as quickly as she had turned into a blur. "I'll call you. Got it?"

Dorrie stands in silent amazement. If only Dave could see this. There would be absolutely no doubt in his mind as to her sanity. If only the fairy would talk to her. There are so many questions she wants to ask her. If only.

Reena has no patience for Dorrie. In her opinion there has been too much contact already. "Git!" she orders.

Dorrie feels so confused she races out of the room as if her life depends on it.

Reena points at the fleeing Dorrie and doubles over with laughter. The knowledge that little ol' her could make an adult human run in fright pleases her enormously.

"That wasn't nice," George comments.

Reena turns expecting to see George. But, he is not there. She knows she heard his voice so she spins full circle. Still, no George. Then it dawns on her. She looks down at the jar. There, seated on its rim, is George.

"Butt out. I'm going back to bed," Reena is still boiling from her encounter with Dorrie. Drifting down to the jar is more like freefall with the mood she is in.

"You know, Reena," George gets out of her way. "Not everyone is going to be like Grams. She was kind and tolerant, really nice."

Reena's nose juts into the air. She tries to give the appearance that George's words do not bother her.

George gives her an analytical look which she notices.

"This is my house. Grams left it to me."

George ponders Reena's words. He concludes they are quite illogical. Unfortunately, he shares his thoughts with her. "Sure, that's why she told us about a trip, put some munchies our jar, coaxed us into it, and then sealed the lid nice and tight. Oh, and did I mention that she then burled the jar with us in it under a stack of quilts in that cedar chest? I do believe I left that out."

Reena winces with each of George's words. They have cut her clear to the bone like a razor sharp knife. She has been living in a state of denial believing that Grams would return. But, sadly that is not the case. And now that she has to listen to, be confronted with the truth about someone she loved so dearly from her friend, George, she cannot handle it.

Reena does not openly, readily display the hurt she is feeling. Instead, every part of her being gives testimony to a stifled rage. She points at his rear end, "When I said butt out, I meant it!"

George's brow rises. He is confused by her behavior. Has she not heard one word he has said? And, then he looks down at the jar's opening. "Oh, sorry," he blushes at being so brunt and absent of chivalry in his actions. He floats off the jar thinking it is best to get out of her way just in case her mood continues to deteriorate.

Reena starts into their home. "That's all right, George," she says in a detached voice.

There is no response from George. He figures that since Reena is in a foul mood, he is already awake, and not only out of bed but also out of their comfy home that he may as well top off his stomach. And, that requires a trip to the kitchen. He can accomplish two things at once; give Reena the space she needs and eat a hearty snack.

Reena glances overhead and sees him leaving the area. "Where are you going?" she asks.

George rubs his stomach, "I'm hungry."

Reena stops in the opening of the jar. She agonizes a few moments then looks at George. It is not wise for either of them to venture out alone with that Dorrie person on the loose. "Oh, okay, we'll go find you something to eat. Then, I'm going back to bed."

George smiles. He really did not want to leave the attic without her.

The fairies float across the attic to the door. George slows his flight pace and waits for Reena to catch up.

"I didn't mean to make you mad," George apologizes too ashamed with his outburst to make eye contact.

"I know. Just sometimes the truth hurts. I thought Grams loved us," Reena hangs her head.

"I thought so, too."

"Until we were left abandoned in the cedar chest," Reena shudders with the memory.

"Some travel by car, some by plane. We always traveled by jar," George chuckles nervously. "How were we supposed to know?"

"It will be okay," Reena limps a smile in his direction.

The two float out the door.

"Food makes everything better. Right, George?"

George grins, "Righty-oh."

Devon and Daryl sneak along the front side of the house. They waited what Devon considered a long enough period of time before doubling-back to the house.

"Dad's at work. Why are we sneaking around?" Daryl asks.

"Mom's still home. You want to do chores?"

Daryl vigorously shakes his head. Somehow he had forgotten that minor detail.

"Okay, then," Devon crouches low. He stealthily approaches the living room window. Once there, he tries to peek through the drapes. But, he cannot. They are still tightly closed.

"Do you see Mom?" Daryl asks nervously.

"Don't see anything." Devon scoots over and checks the front door. He turns away from it.

"What's the matter?"

"Door's locked."

"What?" Daryl stands motionless. His eyes look around as a trapped animal might. "We're locked out? We can't get back in?" he asks with his voice getting louder and shriller with each syllable.

Devon slaps Daryl on the arm, "Door's locked, maroon. Come on. The back door will be open."

"Oh, yah, it's never locked." Daryl follows his brother to the side of the house.

The twins check the windows they pass as they go and keep a lookout behind them. Both come to a quick halt when they get to the backyard.

Reena and George walk along the kitchen counter. Crumbs from a nearby loaf of bread lay scattered at their feet. George grabs a handful and snacks on them. He sees a bowl filled with apples, bananas, and grapes. Reena's eyes follow his gaze.

George points to an apple. "How about?" he asks eagerly. The thought of the large, juicy fruit has his mouth watering.

"No," Reena responds. She parts with him and flies up to check out the cupboards' contents.

"Just one," George almost pleads.

Reena shakes her head. "You can't eat all that."

George's eyes widen, "Sure I can."

Reena opens the cupboard over the refrigerator. She claps her hands enthusiastically and licks her lips. Before her are neatly stored bottles of wine. She pulls one out and transports it to the counter.

"Reena, please?"

"Yah, you probably can," is the only response she gives him. She knows he will eat the apple regardless of what she says.

"Look out below!" George yells as he rolls the apple onto the counter.

Devon spots their mother in the backyard. She is busily tending to a half-dead flower garden. He watches her a few moments before quietly moving to the back door. Once there, he stops and glances over his shoulder.

To Devon's dismay, his brother has not moved an inch. Daryl stands petrified.

Devon whispers, "Move it."

Daryl vigorously shakes his head, "We're gonna get in trouble."

"Not if you're quiet."

Daryl still does not budge an inch. His eyes are fixated on their mother.

"One, two," a miffed Devon stops counting and rushes back to Daryl. He grabs his arm and jerks him into a response.

Dorrie stands and wipes her brow. She has neglected her flowers for several months because of Gram's illness and death.

This flower garden brought Grams great joy. Every spring she had a bountiful harvest of lovely flowers. Grams had a proverbial green thumb. A trait which Dorrie believes she did not inherit even though Grams would spend hours giving her gardening tips. "Time, Grams. We had some very good times out here."

Devon pulls Daryl to the back door even though his brother is acting obstinate.

Dorrie stops. Without turning around she listens. She can feel someone is behind her. And then she hears it, footsteps on the patio.

In the kitchen, George grins as he hugs the apple. Reena, always alert as a good fairy should be, hears shoes shuffle outside the back door.

Daryl, standing close to his brother is near panic, "Mom thinks we went to school. We're gonna get in big trouble.

Devon takes hold of the doorknob. "Not our fault it's Teachers' Day," he turns the knob.

Reena slams the cupboard door shut then quickly flies down to George, "Quick."

"Huh?" George barely looks up from his apple when Reena flies up and pushes it away from him.

"Hurry, George."

George reaches out to his treasured treat, "But, my apple."

Reena snarls at him and grabs George's hand, "Later."

The fairies fly to the top of the refrigerator minus something. George feels the top of his head. His hat is gone. He looks over the edge of the refrigerator down at the floor and sees it.

"My hat," he says barely audible.

"What?" Reena's eyes follow George's extended index finger. "Oh, well, don't you worry about that. We'll get it," she says not knowing when or how they can retrieve it.

"Promise?"

"Yes," Reena says as she pushes George behind the artificial plant.

The fairies no sooner duck behind the plant than the boys slip into the kitchen.

Dorrie turns but not in time. She gazes at the patio, "Mm. Great. Now I'm hearing things, too."

Reena peeks around the plant and watches as Devon and Daryl scurry through the kitchen toward the living room. She relaxes once they are through the door and gone. "Okay, they've left."

"They? Who?" a quaking George asks.

Reena frowns, "Their children."

"Oh, my, I'm feeling faint," the back of his hand touches his forehead.

Reena floats down from the refrigerator. "Really? Then I guess I have a new hat." Reena scoops it off the floor and dons it.

George is alarmed. He looks down at Reena and dives in an erratic pattern towards her. She ducks just as he grabs his hat off her head.

She smiles, "Guess all that leaves me is the apple."

"Huh?" Wow, now, he cannot let that happen. After all he had dibs on it. If he remembers correctly she was more interested in that old bottle of wine.

Reena teases him by stroking the apple. George suddenly lands next to her. He licks it.

"Eugh," she frowns and turns away.

George feels ever so much like a conqueror. His hands ravenously dig into the skin. He pulls out handfuls of the fresh pulp and feasts contentedly.

"Disgusting," Reena turns her back.

George is creating quite a mess which she cannot bear to see. Apple pieces and juice splatter onto the counter and him. She does not understand how he managed to get to this stage of his life without learning basic table manners.

Devon and Daryl have made it up the stairs and into the attic. Here they can play for hours without anyone knowing.

"We are so smooth," Devon declares proud of their prowess at evading their mother.

"Yeah," chimes Daryl.

In only a few moments the boys transition from fleeing like fugitives to that of playful boys. Finding two broom handles propped against the wall helps. After all, these are not just any broom handles. These are swords.

Devon grabs them and tosses one to Daryl. "Pirates," he announces.

Daryl examines his "sword". It meets with his eight year old tastes for balance and strength.

"Aye shall defend her majesty's prized jewels with me life," Daryl thrusts his handle towards the ceiling

Devon extends his handle toward his brother, "Ye shall have to fight to keep them."

"Fight ye I shall," Daryl declares.

"I shall steal these treasures that ye've kept hidden all these years," Devon laughs wickedly slapping his handle against Daryl's.

"No!" Daryl lunges at Devon.

The broom handles clash as the boys move further and further into the attic.

"Surrender the jewels," Devon commands.

"No."

The two bat their handles about for several minutes.

"Then it shall be your death," Devon suddenly lunges at Daryl.

Daryl is caught off-guard and loses his balance. He falls into the dresser with a loud thump.

Dorrie approaches the back patio with garden tools in hand. She cocks her head a moment, stops, and listens intently. A bump is heard coming from the open attic window.

"No," she drops the tools on the grass.

Devon bats at Daryl's handle with such force he takes his brother by complete surprise. Daryl's handle is knocked free from his grasp. It drops to the floor.

Daryl watches in horror as the handle bounces across the floor out of his reach.

Devon smiles triumphantly.

"Then my death it shall be," Daryl says with resignation.

Reena jumps, "What was that?"

"Huh?" George only hears the slurping noises he is making with the apple.

Reena moves quickly toward the living room.

Daryl tries a futile attempt to regain his "weapon". He lunges for the handle.

"Die," Devon quickly brings his handle up blocking Daryl.

Daryl's eyes plead with his brother to no avail.

Devon delights in winning, showing his twin who is the better of the two. He pushes Daryl onto his back then drives the broom handle toward Daryl's chest as one would an enemy on a battlefield.

Daryl lets loose a loud, blood-curdling scream and immediately closes his eyes. The end of Devon's broom handle is only a few inches from his chest.

Devon laughs and struts over to the dresser. He leans against it, "Steal ye treasures, now, I shall."

Daryl does not respond. He is pretending to be dead.

Devon opens and closes each drawer. Not so much as a dust bunny is available for his pretend treasure. He is disappointed but undaunted in his quest for the pretend treasure. And then he notices it. The dresser is pulled away from the wall.

He tries to push the dresser back but it will not budge. Something is blocking it. Devon tries again. Still, it will not move. Out of exasperation he looks down between the back of the dresser and the wall.

"And, what have we here?" Devon sees the jar and picks it up. He examines it in the light from the window. This treasure meets with his approval so he takes possession of it and proudly strides toward the door.

Dorrie rushes into the kitchen. That noise she heard can only mean one thing, the boys are home. Like Mom, like sons.

Reena and George barely duck behind the fruit bowl before Dorrie enters the room.

"Boys!" Dorrie hurries through the kitchen.

Reena and George walk around the bowl keeping themselves out of sight while maintaining a visual on Dorrie.

Once she is out of the kitchen, George returns to his apple. Only Reena has other ideas and pulls him away.

"My apple," George reaches back for remnants of the fruit.

"You've had enough. Come on," she tells George.

George wipes his face on his sleeve. "I'm not done," he snivels.

Devon, having heard his mother's voice, wastes no time getting clear of the attic. He races down the hall toward the bedroom with the jar tucked under his arm. It is imperative that he put the jar somewhere safe, somewhere she will not readily see it. There is no way she will let him keep this if she finds him with it.

Dorrie quickly ascends to the top of the stairs. She repeatedly calls the boys as she goes. They do not respond.

Daryl finally hears their mom. His eyes pop open. He looks around the room a moment then realizes his brother has already left. He scrambles to his feet and scurries out of the attic.

Devon sits calmly on his bed waiting for their mother. Daryl dashes into the room and hurls himself on the bed just a moment before Dorrie appears in the doorway.

"You're home?" Dorrie enters the boys' bedroom surprised and relieved.

Devon offers an excuse, "Teachers had some kind of a meeting."

"Are you sure? There was no note written on the calendar."

The boys shrug, shake their heads.

Dorrie looks around the room suspiciously. "So, you came home and are just sitting quietly on the bed; in the middle of such a beautiful day?"

The boys nod in unison.

"Well, that's really good to hear. That gives you both the time you'll need to clean your room."

The boys look at each with shocked expressions covering their faces.

"I need to run to the store but I've got to clean up first," she adds.

"Okay," Devon responds nonchalantly.

"You two stay in the house and work on this room."

Again Devon is pleasantly agreeable, "Kay."

Dorrie stares at Devon a long moment. "Nice to know everything is fine," she says not believing a word of it.

"Yes, Mom," Devon answers.

"Okay. I won't be gone too long." Dorrie steps out of the room.

The minute she is clear of the doorway she mumbles under her breath, "You two are up to something. Never are quiet or in the house on a gorgeous day. Totally out of character for the two of you."

Daryl slaps his forehead, "Well, that's just great."

Devon gets up and walks over to the closet. He, unlike his brother, is not worried about what their mother said.

"Where do I start?"

"Start what?"

"Cleaning?" Daryl looking at his belongings.

Devon shakes his head. "Mom always tells us to clean our room and we don't and then she gets busy and, that's the way it is."

This had not dawned on Daryl. He smiles knowing his brother is right. "Yah."

Reena and George left the kitchen and returned to the attic only to find to their horror their home is gone. They hover above the dresser.

"Where did our home go?" George woefully asks.

Reena is at a loss. It did not just get up and walk out of the room by itself. Someone would have had to take it.

George takes a seat on the dresser. "My comfy bed. How am I supposed to take a nap?" he mopes with his head cradled on his hands. Then it dawns on him, "All our munchies are gone!"

Panic takes over. He rises to his feet and paces the top of the dresser. His hands intertwined behind his back.

This is more than Reena can bear. Their home has vanished along with George's favorite comfort foods.

Devon opens the closet door in the boys' bedroom and pulls the mason jar off the top shelf. Daryl, curious as to what his brother is up to, joins him.

"A jar?" Daryl asks.

"Pirate's treasure, matie, discovered in the deepest parts of yonder attic," Devon twists the lid off.

Daryl takes a step back.

"Chicken," Devon chides.

Daryl, offended by his brother's label, subconsciously puffs out his chest, "I'm not a chicken."

"Sure, mister bravery in action. I forget, you're just a maroon."

"Am not."

Devon smiles, "Sure." His attention returns to the jar in his hands. He finds the lid relatively easy to remove.

"Let me see," Daryl eagerly approaches.

Devon peeks inside the jar. "Oh," he remarks not knowing what to make of its contents.

"Let me see," Daryl repeats himself.

Devon holds the jar out for Daryl.

Reena flies down the hallway in quest of the fairies' home. She passes the boys' open door on her way to the staircase.

Daryl tentatively peeks into the jar. "What's that?" he points to the inside of the jar.

Devon jiggles the jar, "That?"

A startled Daryl jumps back.

Devon laughs, "Scaring you is always so easy."

Reena comes to a rapid halt. She hovers in the hallway a moment and listens. It is the boys she hears. Zip! She does an immediate about face.

"What are we going to do with it?" Daryl asks Devon.

Devon shrugs.

Reena appears in their doorway. Her tiny body is tense from head to toe. Her face is twisted in rage. She screams at the sight of Devon holding her home.

Devon, startled by the sudden ear piercing noise, drops the jar. Its precious contents of golden dust, cotton balls, and food pieces spill onto the floor.

"No!" Reena yells whisking the jar away.

The boys are stunned, "What the?"

"Bad boys. Bad, bad boys," Reena scolds.

The dumbfounded twins watch with their mouths gaping open as Reena flies the jar out of their room.

Daryl blinks then stammers, "It, it, talks."

A moment later both boys spring to their feet. Their bodies cross the threshold of their room just in time to catch a fleeting glimpse of Reena flying towards the attic. They exchange wide-eyed looks of confusion not knowing what to make of the fairy they have just seen.

Devon and Daryl turn around shaking their heads. They are experiencing a stage of shock which comes from seeing something which is not supposed to exist.

Daryl is first to speak. Only when he does it is not about a fairy. "Uh, oh," he mutters eyeing the debris. "Mom is gonna get so mad."

"Okay, we'll take care of this and then we'll go find that thing," Devon says.

The boys make quick work brushing the jar's furnishings under the nearest bed. It just happens to be Devon's bed which is the closest. After a few moments they realize that try as they may they cannot get rid of that last bit of dust. For anyone who knows it is there on the floor it is easy to see.

A frustrating moment later Devon decides, "She'll never notice. She won't even see it."

Daryl is doubtful but he is not going to argue. Why should he? If there mother does see it she will scold Devon. After all, the dust is under his bed.

The boys dust their hands off and leave the room. Time to hunt a fairy.

A moment later, Reena flies in with the mason jar. She had waited behind an armoire in the hallway until the coast was clear. Now, it is time to reclaim the fairies' property and get their home back in order.

Reena enters the bedroom. Following the dust trail from the floor to under Devon's bed is easy. It is what she discovers underneath the bed which she finds difficult to handle. It is downright appalling.

The dust bunnies, dirty clothes that reek, and dishes with crusted food lie scattered before her. She carefully picks her way through the mess and sees something even more horrific. This element of her discovery leaves her nauseated. It is the state of the fairies' furnishings.

Not in all her years has Reena ever encountered people who so callously disregard their home's accoutrements. It does not matter to her that she and George have had very limited exposure to people. The fact of the matter is every one should have some common thread of decency. To her sorrow, it is more than apparent these boys have none.

Reena painstakingly pushes the mason jar up to the discombobulated pile of golden dust, cotton balls, and bits of food. She kneels at the pile's edge fuming on the inside.

"Bad, bad boys," she declares. Slowly and thoughtfully she gathers a handful of dust and sifts it through her fingers repeating, "Bad, bad boys."

George has been searching room to room in the upstairs part of the house looking for Reena. Devon and Daryl's room is the last room to check before he takes his quest downstairs. He peeks around the corner of the doorway giving the room a quick visual scan. What he sees pleasantly surprises him.

Dorrie is dressed and ready to run her errand. She hears the sounds of rapid footsteps descending the stairs just as she passes the base of the staircase. Unfortunately, before she can turn her head to look, the boys almost mow her down. This was a near collision none of them were expecting.

"Oh, crap," Devon says as the boys flee out the front door.

"What's going on?" she calls after them.

Reena pushes the filled mason jar out from underneath the bed. "Whew!" she wipes perspiration from her brow.

"Our home!" George exclaims from the doorway. Elated, he floats over to Reena, "What a beautiful sight."

Reena dusts herself off. She is covered from head to foot in dust bunnies, lint, and no one knows what minions of germs have latched on to her.

"You found our home. You found our home," George excitedly repeats.

"Slightly remodeled," she replies. The meaning of this goes right over George's head. After all, he was luckily spared from witnessing the travesty which the twins had committed against their little home.

Both fairies are overjoyed to have it back. And, both shall endeavor to find a safer place for their home's next location. The finer details such as that of interior decorating of their humble home are the least of Reena's concerns right now. The little fairy has to take care of one minor detail before she leaves the boys' room; payback fairy style.

A highly agitated Dorrie hurries out the front door yelling after the boys, "You're grounded."

Unfortunately by the time Dorrie steps outside, she no sees no sign of the twins. Several long minutes pass as she looks up and down the sidewalk running in front of the house. Nothing. It is as if the boys have disappeared into thin air.

Dorrie throws her hands up in disgust and turns to reenter the house. It is at that moment she catches a glimpse of Devon's head on the other side of her car in the driveway. She smiles. "These boys just don't learn," she thinks to herself.

A quick trip through the house, out the back door, and around through the backyard to the side of the house brings her up behind the boys. "Inside now!" she announces her arrival.

The boys almost jump out of their skin.

"How'd she do that?" Daryl wonders.

"She always does that. I told you," Devon slaps Daryl.

"Don't hit me. I said she could see you," Daryl slaps back.

Devon slaps his brother on the arm, "Don't hit me. I wasn't the maroon who chose this spot. You were. You always choose this spot and she always finds us."

Devon and Daryl continue to argue as they make their way back to the house.

"Oh, yeah, well who said you could follow me?" Daryl retorts.

George cocks his head. He has a quizzical expression. "What are you doing?"

In rapid succession Reena's activities become more than a little bit clear. She hands the jar off to George, "I've got something to do."

George shakes his head.

"Come on. Now go, take it," she tells him.

George hesitantly takes the jar. He does not leave the area, though. Curiosity causes him to linger just on the other side of the threshold.

Reena begins to spin until she is at full speed. In rapid sequence, the closet's contents float out of the closet and into the toy box. Toys jump to life and move into the closet. Dust bunnies, dishes with dried foodstuffs, and dirty clothes appear from under Devon's bed. Devon's bed sheets pull off the bed.

George watches in amazement. The bed sheets flow under the bed. Dust bunnies, dishes, and the dirty clothes float up and land on Devon's bed in a heap. The mattress on Daryl's bed separates off the box springs. It is suspended a moment in midair. On a final note, Daryl's mattress walks over and leans against the closet door.

Reena stops, dusts her hands off, and smiles. This is quite an artistic bit of work for one who is usually obsessed with just the opposite, cleanliness.

"I want to learn how to do that," George says in admiration.

"Get your room clean while I'm at the store," Dorrie instructs the boys as they dutifully walk up the stairs.

The boys return to pushing and shoving the moment they are out of their mother's sight.

Dorrie shakes her head. This day has been such a busy one already and it is not even half through, yet. Her planned outing will have to be just a short trip now to pick up only the only necessary items. She gathers her keys and purse from the foyer's table and leaves.

The drive to the store will bring her a welcome reprieve from the strife of the twins' constant bickering. An added bonus will be listening uninterrupted to steady music from the satellite radio. It will be so refreshing for her tired ears.

Reena leans back against the window sill in the attic. Her legs are crossed and she is feeling ever so relaxed. A thoughtful wave of farewell to Dorrie completes the little fairy's feeling of satisfaction for a job well done. Especially now.

Devon and Daryl are in a state of complete shock at the threshold of their room. The pair's mouths gape open, they blink, and then the part which brings Reena the ultimate feeling of satisfaction; they scream. There, before the boys' very eyes, their room has a totally redefined stamp of messy.

"Mom!" comes their blood-curdling scream to no avail. Dorrie has driven out of the neighborhood.

A smiling Reena turns away from the window. Now, it is time to tend to the fairies' little home.

Devon and Daryl cannot work fast enough or hard enough to get their room back into its usual state of slovenly before their mother returns. But, they manage to do it and find they still have time for their next course of action; payback twins' style.

Reena and George arrange the golden dust on the floor of the mason jar. The dust is followed by putting the many food bits and their cotton ball furniture in order.

George stops for a moment. His hands thoughtfully sift through the dust. "Without our dust we will be cold this winter," he laments.

Reena rolls a cotton ball into place, "We still have enough to generate heat."

"We do?"

"Yes."

A very relieved George smiles. "Reena knows everything, she always has the answers," he thinks to himself.

"Here," Reena points to a much larger cotton ball. "I'm not putting your bed in place. You can do that."

George huffs and puffs. He physically strains under the weight of the cotton ball as he carefully places the valuable item in place. It is much heavier than he remembers. But, well worth every drop of sweat now beaded on his brow. Moving furniture, anything requiring physical effort, is for George, hard labor. That is, except eating of course.

Once the ball is in position George stands back and admires his hard work wiping the sweat from his face. Deep down George misses those days when he lived the luxurious life of an upper-class fairy. This commoner stuff needs to end at some point. Or, at least he hopes it does.

Reena has been watching George's every move. She finds him quite whimsical at times, like now. Unlike her friend, she never had the opportunity to acquire the tastes of or the fetishes of the elite rich. She has always been middle-class, never to poor and definitely not prosperous.

"It's done," she spins onto her bed ready for restful slumber.

George exhales and thinks a moment. Should he or should he not let her know what he is thinking right about? Why not? The worse she will probably do is moan. The poor, little thing looks far too tired to do much else.

"You know what all this work reminds me of?" he finally asks her.

"No, what?" she asks sleepily.

"That burning calories increases appetite."

"What's your point George?"

"Hm, that I'm hungry," he says softly.

Reena hits herself on the forehead. After all these years of living with George she should have seen that one coming.

A quiet moment passes between the two as Reena struggles to get the energy to get back out of bed. And, as George impatiently waits for her to do so.

"Grief," she sighs in resignation.

The side door to the garage stands partly open. Inside, Devon digs through hunting and fishing equipment. It was neatly stacked in a corner by their father a long time ago before he got so busy at the college.

Devon hands off items one at a time to his brother who creates a sloppy pile with them.

"Found it," Devon finally announces after the bulk of the equipment has been moved.

"What?"

Devon reaches down to the last bit of gear and extracts the treasured find, a fish net. "This. Our thing catcher," he displays it to Daryl.

Dorrie enters the kitchen with her arms and hands loaded with grocery bags. She managed to bring it all in the house with one trip from the vehicle, "Now if that isn't a feat I don't know what is."

Setting the groceries on the counter she notices the apple and the apple pieces. She takes great care to make very little noise putting her purse and keys down. Her eyes begin searching the room. Deep down she knows the fairy has been here.

"Reena?" she calls softly. "Did you do this?" There is no response. The room resounds with emptiness except for her.

Dorrie gets a paper towel, gathers up the apple pieces, and tosses them into the trash. "The boys either eat their food or hide it under the furniture," she says barely audible. "Just so you know for the next time you go scavenging food."

Reena and George smile at each other.

George whispers, "Well, that was bloody nice of her to tell us. Don't you think?"

Reena barely nods her head. She is busy watching Dorrie pull milk, meat, and two cans of whipped cream from the grocery bags.

The top of the refrigerator is a very good location from which to spy upon these humans while in the kitchen. From this vantage point, Reena can clearly see everything Dorrie is doing.

"Oh," Reena gasps softly. Her eyes behold the cans of whipped cream. She beams at the sight of the cream. Her mind immediately spins with delightful images of the creative use she will put it to. Oh, if they only knew she would be ousted out of cleaning fairydom.

George eyes Reena suspiciously. Experience has taught him to distinguish the difference in her smiles. And, this particular grin means she is hatching a plan that will ultimately spell trouble.

Unbeknownst to the fairies, Devon and Daryl are waiting outside the backdoor. They will stay there until their mother leaves the kitchen.

Reena and George breathe sighs of relief the moment Dorrie walks out of the room. George more so than Reena since he has been drooling over a banana in that fruit bowl. What other option has been left to him. It was not he who dumped his apple without as much as a "please" or "I'm sorry" before he was finished with it.

And, who should witness the fairies' flight to the counter? Devon, naturally. It was he who was the lookout waiting and cautiously checking the window until their mom left the kitchen. This could not get any more convenient if he had planned it all.

"Shh," Devon tells Daryl before the boys enter.

The back door silently opens.

Whoosh! A fish net swallows Reena and George plus the banana George was admiring.

"It's mine!" George screams out his claim on the fruit as he throws himself on top of it. To protect it of course. It does not occur to him that only he cares.

The fairies find themselves suddenly transitioned from free roaming agents to airborne captives via net. This is a situation which Reena finds most disagreeable. She seems to be the only one. George is focused on his banana.

Devon grips the top of the net. The rest of it lightly swings to and fro from his hands. He leads the way as he and Daryl march triumphantly to the garage with their treasure.

Reena stands defiantly on the end of the banana. Her fist is raised over her head. A full vocabulary of curse words erupts out of her small mouth at the wicked twins.

George busily nibbling on the banana remembers his manners. He pauses long enough between bites to ask her, "Sure you don't want some?"

Reena stops for a mere second to glare at her friend.

"No. All right," George returns to enjoying his food.

Reena continues to curse the boys. Only now she is doing it at a much greater volume.

Daryl covers his ears, "It's making an awful noise Devon. You sure we aren't killing it or something?"

Devon glances at the fairies, "We'll know when we check 'em."

"I say Reena," George licks his fingers.

Reena flashes an aggravated look in his direction. "What is it George?"

George only wishes to inform her, "All that yelling is upsetting my stomach. Do you think you might tone it done a touch?"

Reena collapses onto the banana. There seems to be no use in vocalizing her objections. Plus, it appears that her tirade has only served to upset George's digestive tract. George with a sick stomach is the last thing she wants to deal with.

The boys transport the net into the garage. Once there, Devon drops the net and its precious cargo into an empty bucket.

"Why you putting it there?" Daryl asks looking on.

"So they can't get out while we're looking at them," Devon explains.

"Oh."

Devon ever so slowly releases his grasp of the net.

The top section spills open. This is it, the moment she has been waiting for. Reena jumps to her feet only to find both boys towering over them. She vigorously shakes her fist in response.

"Wow," Daryl, eyes opened wide, is amazed. "What are they?"

Devon pushes Daryl to the side to take a better look, "I don't know." He wags his finger near the fairies, "Hey, you."

Neither fairy responds. Reena has suddenly grown mute and George, well, his mouth is full of banana.

Devon studies them a moment or two then shakes the net enough to knock the fairies off balance.

Reena reacts immediately flying toward Devon at a speed only a highly irritated fairy can reach. She waves her arms wildly and yells, "Boo" as she goes.

A startled Devon jumps back. He inadvertently bumps into Daryl. His poor, unsuspecting brother is knocked over and lands in the pile of fishing equipment.

Reena starts to laugh but suddenly cuts it short. She has come to the realization that this is probably a good time for the fairies to escape. She rapidly descends to George, grabs his hand, and pulls him to the top of the net.

George is oblivious to her motives, "My banana!" He tries to reach back for it to no avail.

And then it happens, just as Reena can feel that breath of freedom the net is jerked out of the bucket and its opening snaps cruelly shut.

George screams as the fairies collide into the netting, "We're gonna die!"

Devon takes firm hold of the net making sure to keep it tightly closed. "They almost escaped," he tells Daryl.

"Whoa. I wanna see," Daryl starts to right himself.

Devon brings the net up to eye level. "You can really talk," he stares at the fairies.

Reena stares back, unflinching.

Daryl picks himself off the floor and immediately tries to take possession of the net. "I wanna hold it.'

"No," Devon spins around to avoid his brother's probing hands.

Reena and George hang on to the side of the net for dear life. The room spins erratically around them.

"We're goners," George agonizes convinced of their fate.

"Stop or I will tell Mom you broke her cookie jar," Devon threatens.

"You did it," Daryl screams in response.

"We both did it. But, she doesn't know that," Devon gives Daryl an evil eye.

"Okay," Daryl holds his hands up signaling resignation to his brother's wishes.

Devon waits a moment to be sure his brother is not faking him out. Once he is satisfied Daryl is on the up and up he holds the net so both can take a good look at the fairies.

"Where'd you come from?" Devon asks Reena.

Reena calmly turns her back to him. George, on the other hand, is scared stiff. He looks like a pudgy statue.

"Can I have one?" Daryl asks Devon.

"No."

Daryl points to George. "I want that one."

George blinks at the realization that Daryl is speaking about him. He immediately begins to tremble.

Daryl notices the change in George right away, "It's moving."

Reena steps in front of George. "He, not it. He," she corrects them.

Devon whispers to Daryl, "You can have it, him."

A wide-eyed Daryl yells, "Yeah."

Devon loosens his grip of the net. Without warning he callously and quickly brushes the fairies to the side.

"Watch it!" Reena objects.

Devon pulls the banana out from under the fairies removing it from the net.

George objects as strongly as he can (considering he is not exactly the bravest fairy on the planet), "Reena, he's stealing my snack!"

"Bad boy," Reena scolds Devon.

Devon smiles wickedly then tosses the banana in the trash. "Can't have that stinking up the place," he tells Reena.

"Let us go," she calmly responds.

"No," Devon is adamant.

"Please, I don't wanna die," George falls on his knees and pleads.

"Get up George," Reena commands pulling her friend to his feet.

The boys point and laugh thinking these little things are quite a comical sight. Reena and George ignore them in turn.

Devon winks at Daryl. He then informs the fairies, "You're not going to die. We're going to trade you."

"Trade?" Reena's eyes almost pop out of her head.

Devon's eyes narrow, "Yeah, but before we can do that we need to know what you are? Some kind of a windup or battery operated toy? A voice activated something?"

"I got it," Daryl inserts. "They're like my remote control car."

"Where's the remote?" Devon mocks Daryl.

"Oh, yeah," he had not thought of that part.

Reena mumbles under her breath in frustration, "Fairies." Unfortunately, she does not realize at first that she has spoken the word with just enough volume for the boys to actually hear her. That is, until she hears them repeat after her.

"Fairies," the boys say in unison.

Reena sighs in disgust with herself. She wishes she had kept her mouth shut. But, that is not an easy task for her. The little fairy has always been prone to saying what is on her mind.

"We can trade them for my new dirt bike," Daryl says excitedly.

Devon shakes his head. He believes he has a much better plan, "We can sell them on EBay for money. Then we can buy what we want."

"Like a new bike?"

"Mm, hm," Daryl nods.

The boys' plans will have to be put on hold. They hear their mother calling them to come into the house.

"Where we gonna put 'em?" Daryl looks around.

Devon swoops up the net and places it in the large, rubber trash can. "In here. Get the lid."

Daryl takes off the lid and holds it while Devon drops the net inside and then collapses the pole.

The fairies immediately vocalize their objections to the foul odor of the grease laden rags they have landed on. But, neither of the boys pays them any heed.

"We're gonna suffocate," George whines to no avail.

Reena holds her nose closed nodding in agreement.

"Okay," Devon tells Daryl. "Put it on tight."

Daryl replaces the lid and then sits on it till he hears it pop in place. "There."

***

Day has faded into night. The little fairies are still trapped in the trash can. Untangling themselves from the netting has been a bigger challenge taking far greater effort than they have been able to muster so far.

It is bad enough that they are surrounded by used, greasy rags but the fairies also have to deal with Reena's legs poking through the net and George's trapped wing. And, this does not include the raging headache the grease odor has caused poor little Reena.

They both know they must get out of this rubber prison soon. Otherwise, she fears her head will explode and George, well, George always has the same recurring fear — no food. But, neither George nor Reena can help the other until one of them is free.

Each time Reena moves her feet in attempts to free her legs; she has felt icky grease oozing into her shoes and up her legs. This whole scene is far more than she feels she can bear. They must get out of this awful place soon, very soon.

George's eyes plead with Reena. "My wing is stuck," he pulls gently on it from several directions.

Reena extends her hand once again but still cannot reach him.

George gives an aggravated tug to his wing and instantly wails, "It's pinching. Ouch, ouch, my wing, my little wing. I'm going to die with my wing is going to fall off!" He hangs his head in deep despair.

That does it for Reena. They are getting out of this place. She places both hands on her right thigh and pulls with all her might. Finally, after all these horrid hours her leg breaks free. Bop! The opposing action sends her foot flying forward right into George's nose.

"Sorry," she apologizes.

George rubs his nose. "Sure," he says carefully watching her as she works on her other leg. This time, though, when Reena's leg comes free he ducks to avoid getting clobbered a second time.

Reena wastes no time. "Grab that piece," she points at a section of net to his left.

Both fairies take good grips of different sections of the net. Then, at Reena's command, they pull simultaneously in opposite directions.

"More," she encourages George. "He must pull harder or this will not work," she thinks to herself.

George groans, "Okay."

What feels like hours later, Reena and George suddenly fall forward into each other. George's wing has been freed from entanglement.

"Oh, little wing," he joyfully strokes it. "Look, it's only got a couple of creases and one wrinkle."

Reena, excited by his good news, claps her hands. It takes her a few minutes to realize the byproduct of their effort. She and George have been so excited over his wing recovery (it could have been permanently damaged but was not) that neither of them noticed a significant change in their situation. A large whole was created in the net when they had freed George's wing.

Reena stares in amazement.

"What's that?" George asks rubbing his wing.

"Freedom," Reena is ecstatic. "Come on George, we're blowing this dump."

The fairies carefully pick their way through the opening with Reena leading them. Once they are on top of the net, they shimmy up the pole to the lid.

Reena is quite proud of George. He manipulated the pole with no problem. "That was very good George. You have a hidden talent."

George blushes.

She clears her throat. "There's no time for modesty. Come on, help me push this lid off."

"Right." George regains his composure. It has been so long since Reena complimented him about anything that he did allow himself a few moments to bask in the glory of it.

The fairies pop the lid open in a flash. It drops to the floor almost noiseless. After all, it is made out of dense rubber.

"Wee hee!" yells one very happy George.

Reena spins, elated they are no longer trapped in that horrid can. Until she takes a good look at her legs and feet. "Oh, I hope this doesn't stain."

Meanwhile inside the house, Devon and Daryl carry on whispered conversations at the dinner table between mouthfuls of food. The subject of their discussions is, of course, the fairies.

"I want to go to the garage," Daryl states.

Devon's lips barely move as he tries to calm his brother down, "Later."

Daryl moans in response.

"What's that, boys?" Dave asks having heard Daryl's moan.

"Oh, nothing," Devon kicks Daryl under the table.

Daryl glares at Devon then kicks back.

"Stop it, boys. No need to be doing that especially not at the table," their father reprimands them.

The boys lock eyes as they desist from kicking each other. It is their silent vow to one another that as soon as they are out from under the scrutiny of their parents, they will settle their differences, their way.

Dave looks at the boys' plates as he pushes his own away. "How about dessert fellas?"

"Yah, dessert," Daryl is first to speak up.

"Devon, you interested?" Dave asks him.

"Sure," Devon responds curtly.

"All right then. Let's ask your mother if the pie is ready." Dave turns his attention to Dorrie.

Dorrie has already left the table and gone into the kitchen. There is a nice pumpkin pie sitting on the counter waiting to be eaten.

"Hon, looks like everyone is finished eating dinner," Dave rises from the table to help Dorrie. "I believe there's enough room left in my stomach to fit a nice slice of that pie."

"I picked up some whipped cream at the store today," she reaches into the refrigerator.

Dave walks up behind her. "I'll take the plates and pie to the table."

Dorrie stands in front of the open refrigerator door and stares.

"Something wrong?" Dave asks walking away.

She closes the refrigerator door and joins the family at the table.

"Where's the whipped cream? I thought you were getting it," Dave asks her.

"Need me to get it?" Dave asks rising from the table.

Dorrie looks perplexed. She looks at Dave and then at the boys, "Sure, if you don't mind running to the store to pick it up. Seems I forgot it today."

Dave sits back down, "That's all right." He scoops a big slice of pie onto his plate. "Guess we can eat it without the whipped cream. Right sons? We're men, we can tough it out."

Dorrie dishes up the pieces of pie for each twin.

The boys make faces at the pie. Just the thought of consuming pumpkin pie straight makes them feel nauseous. Eugh is the word which sums up their feelings on the subject.

"Well?" Dorrie asks her sons. "Aren't you going to eat it?"

The boys nod. They have a choice. If they eat slowly the taste of the pie will linger in their mouths and it will take longer to finish. But, if they eat fast, they will be done in just a few minutes.

Devon and Daryl make brief eye contact. They then begin to take as big of bites as possible, only partly chewing each one before swallowing.

Each mouthful is excruciatingly hard to force down their throats. The remedy for that are large gulps of milk after every bite of pie. This will help to flush the taste of the pie out of their mouths.

While the family is busy at the dining room table one little fairy is taking full advantage of it. Reena is keeping herself occupied exercising her creative streak in the boys' room.

Daryl's bed sheets rustle lightly as lumps move around between them. A few minutes pass and then the covers pull back just enough to reveal Reena and two empty cans of whip cream.

"Wee hee," she triumphantly transports the empty containers under Devon's bed. The little fairy is quite pleased with her naughtiness.

The boys, finished with their food, head up the stairs. Neither is feeling well enough to be concerned with fairies right now.

"Can you believe it?" Devon asks gripping his stomach in disgust.

Daryl climbs the stairs on the heels of his brother. "Man, straight pumpkin pie. It was awful. I think I'm gonna be sick."

Devon scowls at Daryl, "Me too."

Daryl suddenly covers his mouth. A wretched sounding burp erupts. He runs up the last few steps and into the boys' bathroom.

Devon goes to their room. He quietly gets ready for bed. "This hasn't been such a great day," he thinks.

The bedroom door opens. Daryl slowly makes his way to his bed.

"You don't look so hot," Devon observes. "Kinda blue."

Daryl changes into his pajamas, "All I'm doing is burping."

"Your stomach still hurt?"

"No."

"Mine either. No more pumpkin pie, ever."

"Me neither," Daryl agrees.

The boys crawl into their beds. Devon gets his head comfortable on his pillows. His brother, on the other hand, feels something wet and sticky and...

Within the space of a few seconds Daryl jumps out from under the covers. His mouth opens wide and a blood-curdling scream erupts that echoes throughout the house.

Devon quickly sits up and looks at his brother.

"What the?" Dorrie and Dave race out of the kitchen.

"Oh, oh, this is too, this is too, too funny," Devon is overcome with laughter.

"Mom!" Daryl bawls. "It's not funny!" he snaps between screams at Devon. Poor Daryl is smeared with whip cream from his shoulders down to his feet.

Devon laughs so hard his stomach ache returns. "Oh, my stomach," he doubles up.

Dave and Dorrie thunder up the stairs to the boys' room. They stop dead in their tracks in the bedroom door's threshold.

"Boys," is all Dorrie can say.

"Riddle is solved. You did buy whipped cream today," Dave stifles a chuckle.

Dorrie is aghast. She starts to enter the room.

"Slow down, hon. They aren't dead or anything," Dave tries to calm his wife.

"Not yet," she snaps in response. "You're no help."

Dave takes another look at the Daryl. He can no longer refrain from laughing.

"Mom!" Daryl screams seeing his father's reaction.

"It will be all right," Dorrie tries to comfort Daryl.

"But, Mom," Daryl snivels.

Dorrie shakes her head at Dave, "You're making it worse."

"Sorry, hon," Dave weakly apologizes swallowing his laughter. "Daryl, get in the shower. Devon, clean up Daryl's bed."

"But...," is the only word Devon is able to utter before he is cut off by his father.

"Daryl, go to bed when you're done." Dave stares at Devon, "I'll deal with you in the morning."

Devon defends himself, "I didn't do it." His words land on deaf ears.

Dorrie smiles up at her husband. It has been such a very long time since he last took an active role in the family. She reaches over and touches his arm, "Thank you."

Dave smiles back at her.

"I'm going to help them. Otherwise, these boys will never get to bed." Dorrie is stopped before she can act.

"That's all right. I'll supervise them. You go relax. Past time I got re-involved with my family," Dave responds.

"It's nice to have you back," she whispers in his ear.

Dave watches as she leaves the room. He then looks back at the boys. He is still struggling not to break out in full laughter at the sight of Daryl.

Reena is taking it easy in the den while the family deals with her present to the twins. She happened across a book on a shelf which caught her eye. It turned out be quite an engrossing of literature for her.

The book is not just any book. To Reena's limited understanding about the world it appears to be an authoritative guide on her favorite subject, fairies.

Dorrie makes her way down the stairs. She is going to check the house, make sure the doors are locked and the lights are turned off. Her first stop will be the den.

As she passes through the living room she notices the light on. "Dave," she thinks to herself. He spends some portion of every evening in the den and usually forgets to turn it off when he is done. It does not dawn on her that the room sat in darkness just minutes ago when she and Dave had passed by it in response to Daryl's screams.

Reena hovers over the opened book which she placed on the coffee table. She is totally engrossed in its every word and the pictures on its pages.

"Oh, no," she suddenly stares in disbelief. Her hands clasps her cheeks, she stops, gasps, and then blinks. Surely what she has just read cannot be true.

"I'm not real," she mutters as her whole foundation of belief is shaken to its very core.

Dorrie's fingers touch the light switch when her eyes happen upon none other than Reena. Her mouth drops. There, hovering above the table is Reena. She stares in wonder at the tiny creature.

Dave, having gotten the boys to settle down, is walking down the stairs. His footsteps on the landing snap Dorrie back to that moment when her husband had, for all intents and purposes, called her a loon.

Dorrie quietly backs out of the den. "I'm going to leave this for mister psycho babble," she thinks to herself.

Dave walks up to her. He looks at the den and then at Dorrie. "Oh, guess I left the light on again. Sorry."

"And, your mother said you were housebroken," she smiles. "Thought you were going to supervise, Dad," she looks him up and down.

"They're fine." Dave steps up to the den's doorway. "I can turn it off. I left it on, I can turn it off."

"No, not yet," Dorrie shakes her head and steps away.

"You going in there?"

Dorrie smiles and looks toward the room, "No, Reena is reading a book."

"What did you say?" he cannot believe his ears.

"Reena is reading." Dorrie turns away from Dave, "Take a look for yourself."

"Oh, here we go again. Enough already." Dave takes one step into the den and immediately stops in his tracks.

Reena looks up from the book at the same time that Dave sees her. She smirks at him then returns to reading.

Dorrie patiently waits for Dave to apologize. Now would be a good time. After all, here he stands with evidence right in front of his own eyes. To her disappointment, an apology is not immediately forthcoming. Instead, Dave hurries out of the den in shock.

"You thought I was crazy," Dorrie follows him.

Dave pulls her into the other room. He glances back at the den before he speaks. "Reena, a fairy," his voice is filled with uncertainty. "There is a fairy in our den."

Dorrie nods with a smug look on her face. "The one you said doesn't exist."

"She can't. There are no such things. They are myths, folklore, you know, make believe."

"Maybe you should tell her that. Because from what we've both seen, she is quite real."

Reena hears the couple's voices and leaves her reading to investigate. She hovers out of sight nearby listening intently to every word of their conversation.

"No, no," Dave shakes his head and begins to pace. "There has to be a logical explanation to all of this. Fairies," he stops. His eyes search Dorrie's face. "Fairies do not exist."

Reena's wings droop. A frown traces across her tiny face.

"She does too," Dorrie insists. "You saw her with your own eyes."

Reena's ears perk up.

"No, I saw something. No. I think I may have seen something," Dave stresses the word think as he stammers. His mind is reeling trying to find a reasonable explanation for what he witnessed.

Appalled, Reena tenses. First that book said she does not exist and now this man does not believe in her either.

"Who cleaned the kitchen? I didn't, you didn't, and Heaven knows the boys didn't."

"Maybe it's the stress from Gram's passing. Maybe it is beginning to affect me in that way too," Dave is cut off before he can finish what he was going to say.

Reena flies up to Dave. She does it in plain view making sure he gets a good look at her and then exits just as quickly as she had entered.

Dave, stunned, concedes, "Okay, she's real."

"That's what I've been telling you."

Reena comes back. She flies up behind Dave with her tiny hand formed into a fist.

Dave turns around to go back to the den.

"Watch out," Dorrie catches a glimpse of Reena.

Dave looks back at Dorrie. He does not see Reena and accidentally bumps into the little fairy.

"Oh," Dorrie gasps.

Reena hits the wall. She slides to the floor. Shaken, she stands. Her eyes see stars. She wobbles a bit and then shakes herself all over.

Dorrie approaches Reena to render aide but the fairy has taken to flight before she reaches her.

A very determined Reena forms another fist and quickly flies into Dave's face. This time she makes contact bopping him on the end of his nose.

"What the?" Dave asks surprised.

Dorrie laughs.

Dave rubs the end of his nose and glares at Reena. "Why you," he chases her out of the room.

"Dave, Dave don't," Dorrie runs after them.

The couple comes to a rapid halt at the den's doorway. They stare at each other and then at the room. The light is off and the book has been put away.

Dave takes a step back. "My dear," he addresses Dorrie as calmly as his voice can muster. "We have a choice. Search the house now for something a few inches tall that flies at the speed of light or, wait until tomorrow when there's full daylight and we can see what we're doing."

Dorrie beams, "So, you finally admit there really is a fairy."

A very embarrassed Dave barely nods his head in acknowledgement. Admitting when he is wrong has never been one of his strengths.

"You are insufferable," Dorrie's foot stomps down hard on his.

"Ouch!" Dave yells. "What'd you do that for?"

"For thinking I'm nuts!" she tells him storming toward the stairs.

"Hon, hon wait," Dave calls after her.

Dorrie pays him no heed. She is going to bed now. A restful slumber is guaranteed now that her husband has admitted that she was right. The apology can wait. She feels great satisfaction with his acknowledgement.

It takes several minutes for Dave to hobble up the stairs. He knows from the way his foot is feeling that it will be hurting for several days to come.

Dorrie is already dressed in her nightgown when he enters their bedroom. She does not acknowledge him.

Dave hobbles around to her side of the bed. He sits down next to her. "I'm sorry I didn't believe you," he gently touches her shoulder.

Dorrie lies still, unresponsive. This whole thing of not believing her hurt her very deeply. It is not something that a couple of words can easily repair.

"Will you accept my apology?" he asks tenderly. "I would give anything to undo what I have said but I can't."

Several long minutes pass. Dave stands, his head hung low. He feels Dorrie's hand on his leg.

"I'm sorry, too," she says softly. "It hurt so badly when you did not believe me."

"I know. I really am sorry for doubting you."

"Come to bed, handsome," Dorrie pats the bedcovers.

In the kitchen an empty wine bottle lies on its side on the counter. Reena crawls out of the bottle smacking her lips. She is a drunken mess. Her hair is in disarray and her clothes are wet and stained. She reeks of alcohol.

"She doesn't exist," she repeats out loud over and over.

The room begins to spin wildly through Reena's bloodshot eyes. She reaches for the mouth of the bottle missing it on the first few attempts. When her hand finally grabs hold she uses it to stabilize herself and rise to her feet.

"Whoa," her knees try to buckle from underneath her. She waits a moment then staggers over to the cork and props herself against it.

"Whew!" Reena feels exhausted. Drinking so much wine felt fine at the time but trying to leave the scene of the crime has proven to be quite a workout. She needs rest, sleep.

Reena starts to close her eyes. Rest proves to be an impossibility for now. Her body is overcome with a nonstop barrage of hiccups. No matter how hard she tries for an air of sophistication during the hiccup onslaught, she is just too drunk to pull it off.

Her hand suddenly covers her mouth. But, it is a bit late. From the depths of her being, a loud burp erupts. A sheepish smile traces across her lips.

Wisps of hair fall across Reena's face covering her eyes. She clumsily brushes at them in an attempt to see more clearly through her bloodshot eyes. The first thing she notices is the room. It is not only blurry but is spinning faster and faster.

Reena's eyes suddenly roll back in her head. Her eyelids close. Thump! She has passed out.

George flies down the stairs with great trepidation. His body quakes slightly as he checks the rooms. Just the slightest noise of any type and he slams his body tight into the wall. It is his in an attempt to blend and not be seen. Each time, he realizes it was the furnace coming on, a draft, a ticking clock; nothing out of the ordinary.

In the living room he examines the window and the area behind the drapes. Nothing. Now his exploration moves deeper into the room. Next is the sofa. He probes underneath the cushions and the piece of furniture itself. It is such a disappointment to again find nothing.

"Mm," he scratches his head. Ah, the chair of course, how silly of him. How could he forget the oversized chair? The stout fairy buzzes around and under to discover, yet again, nothing.

So far, George is turning up empty handed finding absolutely no sign of Reena. He is beginning to feel frustrated and perplexed. Where shall he check next? He hovers in the middle of the room and scratches his head.

"Ah, the den." Within minutes he has entered and exited the room with the same results. Nothing.

George's stomach growls in an untimely fashion. This quickly redirects the stout fairy's energies away from his mission to find Reena.

"Mm, food," George rubs his stomach. A moment later he is in-flight to the kitchen. After all, no decent search and rescue mission can ever be accomplished on an empty stomach.

Devon stands impatiently next to Daryl's bed. He has already spent several minutes attempting to wake his sleepy head brother. This is no time for the luxury of sleep. There are fairies to be found.

Devon reaches across the bed and shakes Daryl. Daryl does not respond. So, he shakes him again but with more force. His patience has evaporated.

Daryl moans and rolls over still fast asleep.

"Get up," Devon finally yells loudly in Daryl's ear.

Daryl moans again.

"That does it," Devon yanks the pillow from underneath Daryl's head. Not even this extreme action wakes Daryl who continues to sleep soundly.

"You gotta help me. Come on. Get up," Devon pushes Daryl hard.

Daryl finally stirs moaning an almost inaudible, "No."

Devon is persistent. He grabs hold of Daryl's pajamas and drags his poor brother onto the floor. "Get up," he orders.

George pushes the kitchen door open slightly. He peeks into the room and gives it a quick visual. A moment later he cautiously flies in.

"What was that?" he whispers to himself.

George stops and listens. What is that sound he hears? "No, it can't be," he thinks out loud.

Deep down, though, George knows full well that what he is hearing is undeniably a snoring Reena.

"Reena?" George tentatively makes his way towards the sound. And, then, before his eyes he sees, "Reena!"

George hovers over his companion. She is lying in a fetal position on the counter oblivious to George's presence.

"Reena!" George comes closer to her.

She continues to snore and begins to mumble a few indistinguishable words.

George gently picks her up from the counter. "Oh, I say there, I think you've put on a few pounds," he comments under his breath. With Reena cradled tightly in his arms so that he does not drop her, he swiftly flies them out of the kitchen.

Devon and Daryl scurry through the downstairs.

"We gotta find out if they are still in the garage and if they are, move them before Mom or Dad find them," Devon explains to his sleepy brother. "I didn't put that whip cream in your bed and I don't think you put that stuff there either. It had to be those fairies."

"What?" Daryl is beginning to wake now.

"Whipped cream?"

"Oh," Daryl rubs the sleep from his eyes. "But, where we gonna put them then?"

Devon shrugs a response. He does not have a clue as yet.

Daryl is so busy shuffling one foot in front of the other that he is halfway to the kitchen before he realizes Devon is not in front of him. He turns around. "Whatcha doin'?" he asks.

Devon does not move. He stares in the direction of the den. Did he just see George?

Daryl walks up to find out what has captured his brother's attention.

"Shh," Devon puts his finger to his lips indicating for his brother to be silent. He then points to the den.

Daryl looks in the direction of Devon's finger just in time to see George carry Reena into the den.

George is so preoccupied with Reena's safety that he has flown right past the boys and did not even see them. Worse yet, he is unwarily leading them to the fairies new neighborhood.

Devon and Daryl quietly follow the fairies at a discreet distance.

***

Daylight breaks over the Sams' household as the twins learn the hiding place of the fairies' mason jar. After the fairies harrowing escape from the garage, the little creatures relocated their home. George and Reena no longer trusted the attic for good reason. Not only had Dorrie discovered their home but the family's two boys had also.

It was in the attic that their home had been discovered twice. The first time their privacy was violated when Dorrie opened the jar and then to add insult to injury, it was rudely dropped on the floor. The second event, which they are determined will be the last, the twins stole their home and scattered their belongings.

The jar now sits on a very dusty bookcase in the den. Here, on the top shelf, it is safely concealed behind a row of books.

George flies Reena into their jar. She is still out cold not even stirring when he lays her on her cotton ball bed. "Good night, Reena," he whispers in a voice filled with worry.

Devon smiles with a wicked gleam in his eyes, "Got 'em."

The boys high-five each other as they pursue the fairies into the den. They quietly approach the bookcase on their tiptoes.

Daryl immediately reaches for the books only to have his brother grab his arm and stop him.

"Not yet," he advises Daryl. "Mom and Dad will be up soon."

Daryl's lips curl into a frown. He slumps to the floor and mopes. He is so tired of his brother always bossing him, always making him do stuff he does not want to do. But, then, his brother is usually right.

Devon sits cross-legged next to him, "We shouldn't have to wait very long. Mom and Dad will get up and ready for work soon. They're always in a hurry to leave the house when they have to work."

Daryl hears his brother's words but still mopes.

Reena wakes with a rude start. Sounds of thunder echo through her ears plus her head is emblazoned with a warring headache. She covers her ears but finds no relief.

Reena sits up ever so slowly. Dizziness overwhelms her. "Oh," she grabs her forehead.

George is comfortably seated on his bed. "Good morning," he tells her. "You don't look so good."

Reena has a comeback for his comment but cannot get it past her lips. A rash of sneezes erupts sending another very excruciating throb through her head. She closes her eyes.

Cashews are piled beside George. He picks one up and begins munching on it. "Do you feel as bad as you look?" he asks her between bites.

Reena grabs her ears and opens her eyes. "Do you have to eat so loudly?"

"Huh?" At first George does not understand what she is getting at. But all it takes it one very harsh look from Reena for it to click. George looks at the cashew in his hand and then at Reena.

Reena maintains a steady bloodshot glare at him.

"Oh, sorry," it now dawns on George that sounds are amplified to his hung over friend. He stares at the cashew with longing in his eyes and licks it. "Better?" he asks.

"Ah, loud slurping as opposed to loud crunching. Of course, it is so much better on my poor head!" she says in disgust.

George smiles weakly and sits the cashew down. His eyes dart back and forth between the nut and Reena. "It can wait," he says without conviction.

Reena cannot bear another second of feeling so wretchedly awful. Perhaps a nice hot shower is what she needs. She wobbles to her feet and straightens her wings.

"I'd lie down if I were you," George touches the cashew.

Reena ignores him. She is staring at the jar's lid. Then, in the blink of an eye the lid pops off. A fast second later, Reena is a blur. She is a ricocheting blur as she flies out of the jar.

"You don't look good enough to fly," George calls after her. His words are unheeded. "Oh, my."

Reena bounces out of the jar and makes her way to the top of the books. All the movement on her aching head has only served to increase the misery she feels. Perhaps resting for a moment or two will help. Rest does not come. Instead, she is overwhelmed with another barrage of sneezes.

The boys, still patiently waiting at the bottom of the bookcase, hear Reena's sneezes. Daryl begins to get excited and starts to stand.

Devon sharply pushes him down and shakes his head. "Not yet."

Daryl lets out a soft groan of displeasure.

A white glove appears on Reena's hand. Her protected index finger lightly swipes the top of the books. She looks at the gloved finger and disgust shrouds her face. It is smothered in a thick layer of dust. "Ah, ah, ah choo," she sneezes again.

Dorrie, in work clothes, enters the kitchen. Right away the wine bottle catches her eye. She looks at it a long moment before tossing it in the trash.

"Good morning," Dave greets her grinning ear to ear. He slept better last night than he had in years.

"Morning."

Dave walks around to the refrigerator and gets out a pint of orange juice.

Dorrie eyes him suspiciously.

Dave shakes the juice vigorously then opens it and takes a swallow. He notices her look, "What's that for?"

"Did we finish a bottle of wine last night?" she asks believing she already has the answer.

"No, why?" Dave responds taking a seat at the counter.

Dorrie is puzzled. This is not the first morning she has encountered an empty wine bottle. "I found another empty wine bottle on the counter this morning," she tells him.

"Another one? As in, this has happened before?" Dave asks.

"Yes."

"Why haven't you said anything before now?

Dorrie shrugs, "I thought maybe you had finished one off and had just forgotten to throw out the bottle."

"Hasn't been me."

Reena starts to fly away from the books when she sneezes yet again. This time, though, instead of just ricocheting off walls and such she begins to spin uncontrollably off balance. She smacks into the walls without slowing down.

A worried George appears at the top of the books. In short measure he spots Reena. "Not good, not good. This is so bad," he says to himself.

Books fly off their respective shelves and cross the room at a furious pace. Within a matter of seconds they lie strewn on the slate floor. The fairies' mason jar home vibrates to the edge of its shelf then tumbles to its fate. It shatters into numerous, tiny fragments.

"Our home!" George cries. He covers his yes. This is almost more than he can bear. Reena is out of control and one of the first consequences has been the destruction of their humble abode.

Pictures on the walls shake violently then crash to the floor.

Dorrie drops her coffee cup in the sink. "What was that?" she asks alarmed at the noise.

Dave does not slow down long enough to respond. He clears the room before Dorrie can come around the counter.

Devon and Daryl seek refuge under the desk. They watch in stunned silence as the floor lamp crashes with a clatter to the floor and an over-stuffed chair tips over.

"Damage control!" George calls to Reena.

Reena does not hear her little friend's plea.

George makes it as far as the top of the drapery rod in his attempt to flee the room. But, all too quickly he finds himself clinging to the rod in a desperate attempt not to get sucked into the pillage. He shakes violently as maintaining his grip becomes more and more difficult with each passing moment. "Not good. Not good," he repeats.

Dave and Dorrie rush up to the doorway of the den. What they see horrifies them.

"Dave," Dorrie looks to her husband as if he has a reasonable explanation for all of this or, at least, a quick solution.

Her husband stands in mute silence not knowing what to make of the scene they are witnessing.

George eyes the couple, "Oh, definitely not good."

Reena suddenly ricochets off the door jam. She almost collides into the couple.

Dave and Dorrie dodge and duck their way into the den.

"She's zinging around like an uncontrollable missile," Dave says finding a little amusement in the disaster.

"Is everything funny to you?" Dorrie snaps.

"Got to admit not everyone has a fairy without a flight plan."

Zing! Reena's drunken flight plan bounces her through the doorway and out of the den.

"Kitchen!" Dave calls out.

The family scrambles out of the den with George bringing up the rear. They barrel into the kitchen on each other's heels only to come to a quick halt.

"Where'd she go?" Dorrie asks.

Dave shakes his head. The little fairy has disappeared from view. "Let's find out. Hon, check the closet," he directs her.

The boys turn to leave only to be stopped by their father. "Boys, search the drawers," he directs them.

"What are we looking for?" asks Daryl.

"A fairy, stupid," Devon pushes him.

"Knock it off," Dave corrects both of them. "This is not the time for another one of your arguments."

Unbeknownst to the family, Reena did not go anywhere near the kitchen. She took the high road, up the staircase to the nearest bathroom. As the family is busy scouring the kitchen she is getting ready to drown her misery with water.

Water gently flows from the sink's facet. Reena watches it a few moments, tests the water's temperature, and then steps under it. This is the small fairy's version of a luxurious shower.

Once she is drenched from head to toe she crawls out of the sink. A nice, fluffy washcloth creates an inviting wrap with which to dry herself. And, yes, a nice hot shower leaves her feeling so much better; especially her head. That is until she looks in the mirror.

Reena screams at the frightful wretch looking back at her. "What a motley mess," she thinks glancing away. "Oh, no," she looks back at the mirror and realizes that she is staring at her own reflection. "More juice."

"Nothing in here," Dorrie calls to Dave from the closet.

Dave has finished his perusal of all the cupboards. "How you boys doing?"

"Nothing," the twins answer in unison.

Dorrie steps out of the closet, "Dave, did you hear me?"

"Uh, oh, yes. Well, uh, check again. Make sure you didn't overlook something. She's got to be here somewhere."

"Maybe she went back to the attic," Devon responds.

A cupboard door closes behind Devon and Daryl with a loud thump. They turn around to see their father staring at them.

"I should have thought of that. Thanks guys. I guess the attic is next."

Devon and Daryl moan.

A moment later Reena boldly enters the kitchen. She flies in a zigzag pattern to the refrigerator. With her unrelenting hangover the family is the least of her concerns.

Dave and the boys immediately spot her. They stand very still waiting to see what she does.

"Dave?" Dorrie whispers from the closet.

Devon and Daryl talk in hushed voices about the little fairy's condition.

"Reena doesn't look so good," Daryl adds following slowly behind her.

Reena approaches the wine cooler.

"Boys!" Dave whispers a little too loudly.

Dorrie exchanges a look with him as a silent reprimand.

Dave meekly smiles back.

Reena struggles with the wine cooler door becoming increasingly frustrated in her attempts to open it. As a last resort, she kicks it hard.

Wha la! The door pops open.

Reena is beyond ecstatic. What she finds is better than anything she ever could have imagined. Twice the number of wine bottles than were there just last night. It does not dawn on her that in her state of inebriation she is seeing double.

Dorrie draws Reena's attention away from the alcohol by calling her name, "Reena."

Reena stops and turns ever so slowly. At first she smiles at Dorrie and then realizes there are two of them. She quickly frowns at the thought. One of Dorrie was too many in her opinion.

"Oh, look at the poor dear. She's so sickly," Dorrie comments to Dave.

Dave waves her off, "She has a hangover for crying out loud."

Reena knows an insult when she hears one. And, Dorrie and Dave have just insulted her. She disappears behind the artificial plant. A moment later, it moves.

The family stares at the plant not knowing what to make of its movement.

Reena pushes the plant closer and closer to the edge. Her intent is to push it off and hopefully hit Dave. Perhaps a good knock in the head will teach him some manners.

"My plant!" yells Dorrie.

Reena's laughter is short-lived. Dave catches plant.

"Good catch," Devon praises his father.

"Yeah, Dad," Daryl chimes in.

Dave sets the plant on the counter.

Reena's eyes narrow. She mimics Dave and Dorrie, "She's so sickly. She has a hangover." And, with that she hurls herself at Dorrie.

"That more than rips it," Dave rushes Reena.

Reena spins about. Not as wobbly as earlier but the results are similar. The only difference this time is the storm of destruction does not last as long. Just long enough.

Fruit is knocked out of the bowl across the counter and onto the floor. Dining room chairs fall over and the artificial plant vibrates across the counter before finally toppling to the floor.

Reena, satisfied with her handiwork, flies in a zigzag pattern to the door. Unfortunately, she is still very hung over which affects her ability to fly. A smooth exit out of the room is impossible.

Whap! Little Reena lands flat on her back on the floor. Her aim was off and she smacked head first into the door frame.

The family rushes up to her but before they can get to her the fairy shakes her self off and wobbly flies out of the room.

Dave reaches out grabbing the boys by their shirt collars at the door's threshold. "Leave her be for now. Your mother and I will take care f this."

The boys instantly panic out of fear for Reena. "No. You can't!" they scream in unison.

Dave's face softens, "We're going to get Reena some help. She is very sick."

Devon and Daryl's eyes dart over to their mother. They look at her a long moment for reassurance.

"That's right," Dorrie nods in agreement. "Reena is sick and needs our help."

The twins exchange nervous looks before Daryl finally nods to Devon. It is his signal allowing his brother to be their spokesperson.

"Okay, Dad," Devon concedes for the both of them.

Dave strokes the top of Daryl's head, "She'll be all right. Go get ready for school."

"Come on," Devon pulls Daryl. "You heard Dad. Gotta go to school."

The boys leave the kitchen at a slower pace than their parents have seen in months, maybe even years.

Dorrie watches as their sons till they are out of sight. "They sure are taking this hard."

"I know they are." Dave looks at the doorway and then at Dorrie, "I think for all our sakes we should both stay home today and help Reena."

Dorrie responds through a brief kiss on his cheek followed by, "Thank you."

About an hour later, after the boys have been dropped off at school, the Sams' car pulls onto one of the town's back streets. The car moves down the road past several buildings. It finally comes to a stop about midway down the block.

Dave looks out the drivers' window at an old brick building. Chiseled on a weathered sign out front are the words 'Mother Séance'.

"This is it," he says parking the car along the sidewalk.

The couple gets out of the car and slowly approaches the building. They hesitate at the door to the shop. Dave takes hold of Dorrie's hand and smiles at her. This is the only reassurance she needs.

Mother Séance, a fifty year-old woman, is a sight to see. Clad in a multi-colored tunic which contrasts starkly with her wild, salt and pepper colored hair; she looks very much like a 1960's gypsy.

Two knocks on the door is all it takes for the couple to find themselves being greeted with hearty handshakes.

"Come in, come in," Mother Séance opens the door wide.

Dave and Dorrie enter the shop and stare at the motif.

There is a large glass table complete with crystal ball. Overhead a ceiling fan quietly rotates. And, surrounding them are psychedelic colored walls and beaded curtains.

Mother Séance leads them to the table and gestures for the couple to take seats. "Please sit down. Make yourselves comfortable. This may take some time."

Dave and Dorrie take seats in uncomfortable silence. Both are struggling to take in the shop's décor, retro 1960's.

"I think the ceiling fan is the only normal looking thing in here," Dave finally whispers to Dorrie.

"Yes, it probably is," Mother Séance not only heard Dave but she responds to his comment as if he meant it as a compliment.

"Sorry," Dorrie apologizes for Dave. "Sometimes he will say things without thinking. Right, honey?"

"Huh, oh, yah, right. Sorry about that."

Mother Séance looks at the pair a long moment with a pan expression. She then joins them at the table. "Let's get started, shall we?"

The room's lights immediately dim startling Dorrie. Dave notices and puts his around her. The couple exchanges looks of uncertainty.

"There's no need to be apprehensive," Mother Séance leans forward in her seat trying to reassure them. Her eyes move from Dave to Dorrie and back again. "It is important that you believe. Otherwise, you are wasting my time and yours."

Dorrie flinches. She feels as if Mother Séance can read her very thoughts.

Dave feels equally uncomfortable. He reaches under the table and places his hand on Dorrie's thigh. She glances at him and smiles weakly.

Both watch Mother Séance with great interest as she places her palms on the crystal ball. She stares into it intently.

Dave snickers. He cannot help thinking that this whole séance thing is nothing more than hocus pocus, a carnival act.

Mother Séance's eyes narrow on Dave. Sitting back in her seat she tells him, "Tell me your problem."

Dave's mouth drops. He knew it. Her very words are telling both he and his wife that she does not have a clue as to the reason they are here. He mocks, "You didn't figure that out with the ball?"

"No, no, I was checking my stocks," Mother Séance smiles at him like a Cheshire cat.

"Oh, yes, right. That's why we're here," Dave retorts.

"Dave," Dorrie tries to calm her husband. But, there may be no calming to be had. This is a very expensive session they are attending and what with the normal monthly costs of upkeep to that aged house she inherited from Grams, Dave may just decide to stop the session.

Back at the house, one very lonely and miserable George sits in the corner of the attic window's sill. In his lap lies a sleeping and snoring Reena.

George stares out the window lamenting, "Our little home is gone. What shall we do? Oh, Reena."

Mother Séance frowns at Dave. "I was only joking. Why do I always get people who have no sense of humor?"

Neither Dave nor Dorrie know what to think or how to respond to Mother Séance's statement. They look at each other then awkwardly chuckle.

"Well," Dorrie glances over at Dave hoping he will explain their situation but he is conveniently looking away. So, Dorrie starts again. "You see, we have, we have a, friend. That has a drinking problem," Dorrie stammers over the words.

"Your problem, it is very big but it is very small," Mother Séance says in a nonchalant response.

Dave cocks his brow. He gazes at the wallpaper.

"You discovered your cleaning fairy," she smiles at the couple.

"Oh, yes," Dorrie feels sudden relief.

Dave's eyes suddenly focus on Mother Séance, "How'd you know?" he asks suspiciously.

Mother Séance smiles as she stands. "Yes, well how I know is a rather unbelievable tale. One that's better left for another time. So, how is your fairy doing?"

Dorrie frowns, "Not well. She has difficulty with a certain beverage."

"She's a lush," Dave does not mince words. "She gets into the wine." He becomes animated in his description, "She wrecked the house this morning."

Dorrie corrects him, "Not the entire house. Just two rooms, the den and the kitchen. Little Reena looked absolutely horrid. So, sickly."

"Oh, my, you must bring her to me right away. Don't delay."

The couple exchange concerned looks.

"We'll get her to you," Dave tells her.

"You've no time to waste." Mother Séance quickly escorts them to the door.

The door opens and Dorrie steps out of the shop. She turns to find that Dave is still inside.

Before he leaves, Dave has one question he needs to get the answer to, "How much is all of this going to cost?"

"Oh," Mother Séance's facial expression reflects her disapproval of his question. "I'm doing this for little Reena, not you."

"I see," Dave suddenly feels quite embarrassed for having asked.

On their way back to the house, Dorrie realizes she had forgotten to secure the wine cooler before they left on their errand. "Hon, I forgot all about the wine."

"At the house?" he asks.

Dorrie nods, guilt ridden.

Dave sighs, "We both did."

Not long after this conversation the couple arrives home. They go straight to the kitchen to secure the wine bottles. But, it is too late. An empty bottle is waiting for them.

Dave drops the bottle into the garbage can and closes the lid, "She went through that in a hurry."

"Where should we look first?" Dorrie asks.

Dave shakes his head.

Dorrie steps toward the door.

"Where are you going?"

"To find Reena."

"No," Dave tells her.

This upsets Dorrie. "No? Have you changed your mind about helping Reena?"

Dave shakes his head. "Not a bit."

"Then what are you waiting for?"

"Time," he smiles confidently at her.

"Huh?" Dorrie is confused.

Devon and Daryl hear their parents return home and seek them out.

"Mom, Dad?" Devon the first twin to enter the kitchen.

"Yes?" Dorrie responds.

Daryl's voice fills with panic, "We can't find Reena."

"Or George," Devon looks as if he is about to cry.

"Their home is all smashed up into tiny itty bitty pieces," Daryl twists his hands together.

"Their home?" Dave asks.

"The mason jar?" Dorrie adds.

The boys nod.

"C'mon," Daryl grabs his mother's hand. "Show you."

Devon and Daryl hurriedly lead their parents to the den. And, what a disaster awaits them.

Books are strewn across the floor, the chair is turned over, all the pictures are scattered on the floor, and the floor lamp is tipped over.

"Oh, this is going to take some time to clean up," Dorrie says feeling despair.

The family carefully makes their way through the room trying not to step on anything.

Devon walks up to the bookcase and points to the top shelf.

"They had a jar up there," Daryl points.

"It's all broken now," his brother adds looking down at his feet.

Dave and Dorrie see the shattered remains of the mason jar.

Dave tries to reassure his sons, "It will be all right."

"How? Their home is gone," Daryl moans.

Dave rubs his chin. After a thoughtful moment he tells the boys, "We'll think of something for the fairies."

"We were able to find someone who can help Reena. Help her get well," Dorrie shares the information with the twins to distract them from what they see.

"Really?" Daryl asks.

"Really," Dorrie repeats.

Dave leans over and whispers in Dorrie's ear, "If it's not too late."

"Don't say that," she whispers back.

Dave's hand touches her shoulder. He desperately hopes they can help the little fairy. At first, earlier in the morning he was not as committed to this. Now that he sees just how much the fairies mean to his sons, he is. He so dearly wants to protect them from hurt. He realizes that if Reena does not get the help she needs, his sons will be badly hurt.

Daryl shakes his head, "But, their home is gone. Where are they going to live?"

"Like I said, we'll think of something," Dave tells them.

"Reena has to get well first before she can really live anywhere," Dorrie tells them.

"Oh," Devon and Daryl leave the room feeling helpless and saddened.

***

That night, an opened bottle of wine is intentionally left sitting on the kitchen counter as bait. It is Dave's belief that after the household grows quiet Reena will pay a visit to imbibe in her habit. His assumption is correct.

Not long after midnight Reena leaves the mason jar. There has been no movement in the house for several hours leading her to believe the family is bedded down for the night. Reena does not exercise any precautions on her flight from the bookshelf in the den to the kitchen counter. This makes for a very quick trip.

The kitchen door swings open and a small little voice is heard. "Yes!" Reena shrieks her delight at the sight of the bottle.

Reena immediately gets a straw from the kitchen drawer and transports it to the wine. "Mm," she hovers over the bottle smacking her lips in eager anticipation.

George enters the room. He did not go to sleep that night. It is his plan to exercise intervention in hopes of deterring Reena from any further drinking. Neither fairy needs more problems with the people who live here. And, Reena's love of wine has created quite a few already.

Reena wraps her lips around the straw and sucks. All she gets is a mouthful of air. She sucks harder. Still no wine moistens her throat. Then it suddenly occurs to her that the bottle is empty.

George approaches her slowly. "Reena?"

Reena, caught off-guard, spins around knocking the bottle onto its side. "No juice," she says in an angry tone.

"Reena," George tries to get her attention off the wine. But, it does no good for his little friend is en route to the wine cooler.

The wine cooler door opens and to Reena's dismay it is empty.

George watches. He sees Reena's mood escalate from angry to furious. "Not good. This is so not good," he says shaking his head.

Above the refrigerator Reena stares down at the empty bottle and then back at the cooler. It suddenly dawns on her that she has been tricked.

It is now two o'clock in the morning and this fairy's gut is wrenching craving wine. She is panicked and infuriated.

Cupboard doors throughout the kitchen swing open. Dishes and glasses leave their shelves and crash to the floor.

George seeks shelter behind the artificial plant on top of the refrigerator. He is trying to keep an eye on Reena and keep a safe distance from the mayhem.

The kitchen's closet door abruptly swings open. Dave jumps out to Reena's surprise. Across the room Dorrie rushes in from the living room. Together, the couple converges on Reena.

Reena is startled, confused, and furious. She flies first toward Dorrie and then toward Dave. This is a careless mistake on her part.

Dave reaches out and snatches her out of the air. He has caught her in his hands. "I've got her," he announces triumphantly.

"Okay," Dorrie acknowledges. She then rushes out of the kitchen.

Reena's fury only mounts. She struggles to get free from Dave's grasp by scratching his palms with her nails. But, there is no reaction from him. It feels more like a tickle to human hands.

"Hurry, hon," Dave calls.

Reena's face twists in pure anger. Her mouth opens wide and then she bites the skin of his little finger. Again, to Reena's disappointment, there is no reaction.

Dave can hear commotion in the other room and calls out, "Hon?"

The little fairy smiles wickedly. She clears her throat and spits squarely into Dave's palm. In the next instant, she is set free.

"Eugh!" he reacts opening his hands. "I hope you don't have rabies." He goes to the kitchen sink and quickly washes.

Reena darts over to the fruit bowl. Grabbing grapes one at a time, she hurls them at Dave.

Dave ducks and dodges the pelting fruit when he hears the vacuum cleaner from the other room. He smiles smugly at the fairy.

"Huh?" Reena holds a grape in her hand. Her head turns toward the noise. Unfortunately for her, she has reacted too late.

Dorrie has already entered the kitchen with the vacuum cleaner. She wields the hose's nozzle taking aim on Reena.

"Look out!" George yells.

Reena and George both scream as Reena and her grape are sucked up the nozzle and into the hose.

Wha whoop! Dorrie places her hand over the nozzle to keep the little fairy from escaping.

Dave shuts off the vacuum cleaner, "Good thinking."

Dorrie winks.

"I'll get this over to Mother Séance's shop," Dave takes the vacuum cleaner from Dorrie. "Stay home with the boys. Shouldn't be gone long."

"At this hour?" Dorrie looks at the clock it is just shy of two o'clock in the morning.

"She did say as soon as possible."

George, still hiding behind the artificial plant, is petrified. He watches as the couple leaves the kitchen with the vacuum cleaner. "Reena," he calls helplessly.

Dave takes the vacuum cleaner straight to Mother Séance's shop. She greets him in the doorway dressed in an over-sized robe, mud on her face, and curlers in her hair. Dave cannot remember ever seeing a woman look so frightful.

"Sorry about waking you up in the middle of the night but," Dave wonders how she could possibly sleep with that goo smeared on her face, not to mention the antenna twisting her hair down to her scalp.

Mother Séance waves off Dave's apology, "That's all right. You've done the right thing. Reena is seriously ill."

Dave sets the vacuum cleaner down and stands to the side.

Mother Séance carefully inspects the vacuum cleaner before opening the lid. "There are those who do not fully understand the severity of excess alcohol in the system. Toxins can build in the body resulting in death. We do not know how long Reena has."

Dave nods in solemn agreement.

"It may already be too late," Mother Séance somberly makes eye contact with Dave.

Dave gets nervous, "I hope not. I promised the boys."

"Never promise that which you do not have total control over," she shakes her head in disapproval with Dave.

"It's just that the boys care so much about this fairy," his voice drifts off.

The vacuum cleaner's bag draws their attention. It is changing shape thanks to its content, Reena. The tiny fairy is throwing a fit and ricocheting off the bag's walls in an attempt to break out. Her battering of the bag is futile.

"Help! Help!" her muted screams are barely heard.

Mother Séance leans into the bag and listens a moment. She smiles then pats it, "Yes, dear, I intend to help you."

That voice. Reena recognizes it in a vague and distant fashion. Somewhere from her past. That voice is from? She grows still listening more intently as she tries to distinguish if it is coming from friend or foe.

The inside of the vacuum cleaner's bag is littered with smashed pieces of grape and dust. Reena's feet are planted on a piece of the fruit. Her shoes are stained along with her clothes and wings. She is covered from head to foot with dust and pieces of grape. Her wings droop behind her. She coughs then sneezes.

Mother Séance leans over the bag. She pokes it to get Reena's attention. "If I let you out of there are you going to be a good little fairy?"

The vacuum cleaner's bag changes shape. Reena's voice is faint. She shakes her fist over her head while blowing locks of hair out of her eyes. "I'll behave all right. Long enough to teach you," she vows silently to herself.

Mother Séance tears a small hole near the top of the bag.

"You sure you want to do that right now?" Dave asks concerned that the little fairy will escape.

"No need to worry."

Reena's head immediately pops up through the hole only to find she is trapped between Mother Séance's fingers. Her mouth opens. She tries to object at the top of her lungs but only a squeak comes out.

Mother Séance shakes her head. "Tisk, tisk," she looks down at the struggling fairy. "I told you I would let you out if you behave."

Reena squeaks again. This time acting as if she will be cooperative with Mother Séance, "Yes, yes."

"All right, but you must behave," she reminds her.

"Are you really sure you want to do that?" Dave questions the gypsy's wisdom of letting an angry Reena loose.

"It will be fine," Mother Séance assures him with a wink.

"Okay," Dave takes a step back. There is no telling how much damage Reena will do to this room.

Mother Séance removes her hand from the bag.

Reena flies straight up thrilled with her freedom, freedom from that awful bag. She darts about the room joyfully for a few minutes. But, it does not take long before she begins assessing the room looking for cracks in the seals of the window, door, and baseboards. To her disappointment there are none for her to find.

Mother Séance and Dave quietly watch Reena's every move.

Reena zips across the room back to the door. She busily investigates all four edges again without a care as to what Mother Séance or Dave thinks. Frustration begins to mount for again, she can find no avenue of escape.

Just as Reena begins to lose hope in fleeing this room and these people, it dawns on her. The vent. Surely it leads to the outside. She glances over her shoulder and smiles smugly at Mother Séance.

Mother Séance smiles back.

Reena looks at the vent then at Mother Séance. She then flies toward it.

"This room is fairy proof," Mother Séance warns the little fairy. Her words are unheeded.

Reena is determined and continues her flight plan to the vent.

Dave suddenly realizes just how adept Mother Séance is at dealing with the problem he dropped on her doorstep tonight. He is highly impressed, "How about that. A fairy proof room."

"Huh?" Reena finally hears those words "fairy proof". She becomes motionless in midair. Her wings droop. A frown covers her tiny face. There is no escaping this miserable place after all. She turns slowly about.

Mother Séance is face-to-face with Reena. She smiles sweetly but her words are harsh. "Bad fairy," she scolds her as she scoops her out of the air.

Reena, sitting in the palm of Mother Séance's hand with head hung low, winces.

"You can leave now," Mother Séance directs Dave.

Reena perks up. She jumps to her feet. A pleading look sweeps across her face.

Mother Séance lightly clasps her hands together before Dave catches a glimpse of Reena. "I'll call you when she's ready."

"All right," Dave reluctantly steps away.

Reena screams. She desperately tries to push her way between Mother Séance's fingers. But, her efforts are to no avail.

Dave slowly gathers the vacuum cleaner, "Okay, then. She'll be all right?"

"Yes. She will be fine."

Dave steps through the door and heads home.

Mother Séance waits until after she hears Dave's vehicle leave before she deals with Reena. "Now, stop that," Mother Séance tells her. "Mr. Sams is not here to help you now."

Reena hisses.

Devon and Daryl have been wandering through the attic since their father left with Reena. They are very worried about George. Neither boy has seen him in absolute hours. And, to make matters more worrisome, neither of them has been able to find the stout fairy.

"He's got to be here somewhere," Devon says.

Daryl shakes his head, "Maybe Dad took him, too."

"You're being a maroon. Why would Dad take both of them?"

Daryl shrugs. "I miss George," he says. "He's mine, remember?"

"Yeah," Devon acknowledges. He then notices the top dresser drawer. It is open; not all the way just a couple of inches. "Come on."

The boys quietly approach the drawer. They peek inside and at first see nothing.

Devon carefully and very slowly pulls the drawer all the way out. To his and Daryl's surprise they find George. The little fairy is curled up in the back corner sleeping fitfully.

"Hey, fella," Devon says.

George does not respond.

"George?" Daryl tries for a response.

George again does not react.

Mother Séance takes a seat at the table. She observes Reena a few minutes.

Reena looks rough. She has been seated on the table in front of crystal ball since Dave left. All she has done is make faces at herself and Mother Séance and, more importantly, remember. How she could ever have forgotten her previous encounters with this gypsy is beyond her. Those were not pleasant times for the fairy.

"Reena."

Reena curls her knees into her chest. She cannot bear to respond to this mean woman.

Mother Séance leans toward her. "You will be home in a few days or weeks," she says softly.

Reena still does not respond.

Mother Séance waits a moment then ups the ante, "Or, months."

There is a reaction. Reena's head perks up. She turns and glares at the gypsy.

Mother Séance rises from the chair and casually steps away from the table. "You miss Grams, don't you?" she suddenly confronts the fairy.

Reena's lower lip quivers.

"So does that family. Grams was special to you and Dave and Dorrie..." Mother Séance's voice trails off.

Reena cocks her head. A tear trickles down her cheek. No one could love or miss Grams more than she. Not even George.

"You live with Dorrie, Dave, and their boys, now." She pauses a moment, "In Grams' house. And, like you they are hurting over the loss of Grams."

Reena's body trembles as she begins to weep.

"Especially Dorrie. She was very close to her Grandmother. Like you."

"No," Reena firmly objects.

"You need to learn to get along. It's what Grams wanted. For all of you to live together. To be a family."

Reena flies off the table. She hovers inches from Mother Séance's ears. "No!" she screams at the top of her lungs.

Mother Séance shakes her head, "You are still one very stubborn fairy."

Reena does not react.

Mother Séance tries unsuccessfully to make eye contact. She pauses a moment then adds, "Well, then, if you don't want to live with the Sams' family, you'll have to live with me."

Shocked, Reena's respirations become shallow and rapid. She almost faints.

Back at the Sams' house, the attic window is closed for the night. Dave has gone from room to room looking for Dorrie. He finally enters the attic and finds the light is on.

Dorrie has been preoccupied in the attic for over an hour. She has a surprise for everyone that she is working on.

Dave looks across the room and sees the furniture pad is in a heap on the floor. "Hon, what are you doing at this late hour?" he asks Dorrie.

Dorrie is standing in the corner of the room in front of the doll house. She opens and closes its doors and windows, runs a dust cloth across it. Lost deep in a world of thoughts, she has not heard her husband.

Dave approaches her, "Hon? What are you doing? It's late."

"Oh, sorry. I didn't hear you," she turns and smiles at him. "Think Reena will like it?"

"I'm sure both the fairies will," Dave smiles. "Very nice. Very nice of you to want them to have it." He places his hand on her shoulder, "I'm going to check on the boys before I turn in. Want to go with me? Something we haven't done together in a very long time."

Dorrie nods, "It is so nice to have the old you back."

The parents enter the boys' bedroom and find their sons fast asleep in their beds.

"They look so calm when they're asleep. Hard to imagine they are the same rowdy boys."

"Yes, it is," Dorrie smiles. She walks over to Daryl's bed.

Dave approaches Devon's. He no sooner touches Devon's covers than his son's eyes open wide.

"You're supposed to be asleep," Dave whispers tucking him in.

"I can't. Dad, where's Reena?"

Dorrie pauses when she overhears her son's question. The whole fairy thing has been so heart wrenching for the family. She listens a moment to hear her husband's answer.

Dave kneels next to the bed. "We'll talk about it when we're all seated together at the table, okay?"

Devon nods slightly. It is so hard for a child his age to wait on anything especially when it is news in regards to something or someone they care about.

"Get some sleep," Dave tucks the covers between the mattress and box springs.

Dorrie straightens Daryl's blankets. "He always kicks his blankets off. Ever since he was just a baby," she says softly.

Dave steps up, stands beside her. A moment passes. "Come on, sweetheart, they're fine," he coaxes her to leave.

Dorrie does not move. Dave looks at her thoughtfully before he realizes she is staring at something on Daryl's bed. "What is it?" he asks.

She points at Daryl's pillow, "Look."

Dave's eyes follow Dorrie's finger. He is amazed at what he sees, George. The fairy, snoring and smacking his lips, is fast asleep on Daryl's pillow.

"Well, what do you know."

Mother Séance's situation, on the other hand, is not so peaceful. It is far too grievous. Reena is giving her a truly unpleasant time. The little fairy has managed to wear the older woman's patience near the breaking point.

Her typically gentle eyes are narrow and focused on Reena. The fairy has been butting heads with her ever since Dave left. They had not even finished their disagreement over where Reena will ultimately live before another argument erupted. This one regards to Reena's choice of beverages.

Reena is adamant that Mother Séance serve her wine. Of course, Mother Séance is refusing to yield on the issue.

"I want juice," Reena insists in an undaunted manner from her cross-legged seated position on the table. "I want juice."

Mother Séance pushes a baby spoon with grape juice toward Reena.

Reena snubs her nose and pushes it away. "I want juice!" she continues to demand.

Mother Séance pushes the spoon toward Reena again. "This is juice."

Reena snarls at Mother Séance then takes to beating her fists on the table. "Juice with bubbles!"

"Juice doesn't have bubbles," Mother Séance explains. She points at the baby spoon. "This is juice."

"No."

"Yes. What you drank is rotten grapes."

Reena is appalled at the thought. She eyes the spoon. A devilish look washes across her face and then she flips it.

The juice splatters on Mother Séance hitting her square in the eye. She is beginning to really lose her temper.

"Not rotten. It's good stuff. Gram's juice."

Mother Séance, wiping the grape juice off of her face with her sleeve, suddenly realizes the basis of Reena's drinking problem, "Gram's drank wine?"

Reena nods her head vigorously.

"Oh, how sad. That must be where you learned it."

"Huh?" Reena is perplexed.

Mother Séance shakes her head in disapproval, "She drank rotten grapes."

Reena scratches her head. She does not understand where Mother Séance is going with all of this.

"Reena," Mother Séance says with sensitivity. "Juice does not have bubbles. Wine has bubbles."

"No."

"Yes."

"No."

"Wine is made of grapes," Mother Séance informs her.

"Grape juice," Reena proudly announces. "I want grape juice." She sits expectantly totally convinced Mother Séance will honor her request now that she has realized where wine comes from.

"That grape juice is alcohol. Alcohol is bad for you. It can kill you, Reena."

"It is grape juice. Juice is good for me. Grams drank juice."

Exasperated, Mother Séance leans in toward Reena. The tone of her voice is quite serious, "Do you know why they call that juice wine?"

Reena cocks her head, thinks for a moment, and then concludes, "Because the grapes cry when they get pushed into the bottle." She makes descriptive hand motions to accentuate her words.

Mother Séance shakes her head. "No."

Reena's brow rises, "Yes."

Mother Séance bolts from the table to Reena's surprise.

The little fairy interprets this as defeat on Mother Séance's part and begins to chant, "I want Gram's juice. I want Gram's juice."

"Enough already," Mother Séance commands her. "You're not getting any more wine. That's why you're here, to dry out."

"No!" Reena screams shrilly then resumes chanting. "I want Gram's juice. I want Gram's juice."

"I'm going to bed now. Suggest you do the same," Mother Séance's voice is worn and growing hoarse.

"Huh?"

The lights go out.

"Your bed is waiting," Mother Séance informs her from the bedroom's doorway.

Reena slowly rises from the table. This battle is not yet over. She still has not gotten her juice and her body is aching horribly from head to toe.

"Well?" Mother Séance asks.

Reena watches and waits.

Mother Séance does not return to the room. So, Reena is forced to temporarily concede. After all, you cannot argue with a person when they are sound asleep.

Reena gingerly enters Mother Séance's bedroom. On a nightstand next to the bed she sees a makeshift bed. It is made from a pencil box and lined with cotton balls.

"Good night, Reena," Mother Séance turns out the light.

Reena is left to fend for herself in the dark. She almost immediately stubs her toe. Hopping around in pain she inadvertently falls into the pencil box. She squeals out of misery, physical discomfort, and frustration. Only silence is returned. This is the most misery she has ever felt.

Mother Séance hears her but chooses to ignore the defiant creature. She needs rest to face that which is coming in the days ahead.

***

The following morning the Sams' family gathers around the dining room table to enjoy breakfast. This was once a vital part of their daily routine which, unfortunately, was allowed to be overshadowed years ago by Dave's career demands. This particular meal is made even more special. You see, the family is not alone.

The Sams' new found friend, George, is also participating in the morning meal. They have created a seating area just for him. He sits comfortably perched on an upside down coffee cup. And like the rest of the family this morning, he too, indulges in scrambled eggs, biscuits, and gravy. Mm, biscuits and gravy are a real treat for him. They are his favorite. One he could eat daily. One he almost missed partaking in today.

Devon and Daryl found George difficult at best to wake from his slumber. Both of the twins were beginning to think they would have to start breakfast without the fairy. George was in such a deep and comfortable sleep atop Daryl's pillow that he did not want to stir.

Never before had George known such luxury as that feather down pillow. It is decidedly better than any amount of cotton balls could ever be. There is a plush softness to it that beckons one into a state of slumber.

Of course, the moment Devon and Daryl mentioned food, George popped right up off the pillow. That is, after he was reassured that he could return to the pillow whenever he so desired. Need I say that he was also the first of the three to be seated at the dining room table? I thought not.

Dave and Dorrie wait until the boys and George finish eating their breakfasts before broaching the subject of Reena.

Devon gulps his last bit of orange juice. Daryl finishes swallowing his last bite of food. The boys then start to rise out of their chairs to leave the table.

"Just a minute, guys," Dave tells them. "We need to talk."

The twins pass looks of dread to each other. Usually when their dad says "a talk" it is a correction for something one or both of them should not have done. The boys know that this can be a long and extensive list at times. They have such creative, mischievous moments that one might consider them to be above average in their hi-jinks skills.

Dave was kept up all night mulling with thoughts concerning how he could best tell Devon and Daryl and George about the severity of Reena's illness and how long they anticipate her to be in rehab.

"Just tell them," Dorrie finally told him in the wee hours prior to dawn. It is not that she has no concerns for the reactions the three might have. Instead, it is the simple truth of the matter. This is information they not only have the right to know but also have the need to know. And, she was tired, very tired. It was a restless night for both of them.

Dave pushes his plate away. He then looks at the boys, into their faces. This is a mistake for he sees trusting faces looking back at him. Suddenly, despite all his mental rehearsals, he is at a loss for words and an uncomfortable silence falls over him and everyone else at the table. Dave casts a silent look at Dorrie. It is one seeking support.

Dorrie smiles softly. "Dave?" she tries to spur him.

"What?" Devon looks at each of their parents. His eyes finally coming to rest on their father.

At Mother Séance's shop life is not as peaceful. Unlike her friend, George, Reena had a very fitful sleep. It was actually worse than getting no sleep at all. What seems like the space of only a few minutes has actually been the entire night.

Mother Séance, still in bed, reaches over to the nightstand. She nudges the pencil box with her index finger, "Reena, time to wake up."

Reena does not respond.

Mother Séance nudges the box again, "Reena, time to get up."

There is still no response from Reena.

"Grief," Mother Séance mumbles making herself get out of bed to check on the pencil box. After all, she is assuming the little fairy is in there when there is a possibility she may not be.

Mother Séance hangs her weary head over the box. "Mm," she stares down at the fairy. "Wake up, Reena."

Reena moans.

Mother Séance nudges the box again but more sharply than before.

Reena is jolted. "Will this nightmare not end?" she asks herself.

"Wake up, Reena."

Reena forces one eye open. Through the bloodshot view she is appalled to see Mother Séance standing over her. The little fairy immediately curls up into a fetal position. This was not a bad dream after all.

"I'm going to stand right here and continue to call your name until you get up," Mother Séance tells her firmly.

Reena contemplates the thought for a whole second. Being stared at by that hideous gypsy coupled with that wretched sound of her voice would be real torture. Reena can do a lot of out-of-the-ordinary types of things but turn off her hearing, she cannot. She is left with no choice other than to get out of bed.

Mother Séance takes a seat on the edge of her bed. She waits a few minutes until she is sure Reena is wide awake and will stay that way before she, herself, returns to bed. The gypsy is feeling far too tired to deal with a fairy who has an attitude this early in the morning.

Reena slowly pulls herself out of the pencil box. She staggers around on the top of the nightstand trying to get a bead on the bathroom. There it is, across the room. Reena musters up to go airborne. A sink shower is in order. It will help her feel better.

A few minutes later, a refreshed Reena reenters the bedroom. She is stunned by what she finds. Mother Séance is back in bed. Not only is she back in bed but she is also sound asleep. Reena is infuriated.

Meanwhile at the Sams' house, Dorrie picks up the slack left by her husband's sudden state of speechlessness. This should give him a moment to regroup. Dorrie is, for lack of a better term, breaking the ice.

Dorrie starts by asking the boys, "When one of you needs help, we make sure you get the help you need, right?"

Devon and Daryl nod. Both are wondering what this has to do with breakfast or school or their planned after school activities. George is also listening intently, that is between bites of what was an untouched biscuit.

"And, I think we all realized Reena needed help. Right?" Dorrie adds.

"Yah," Devon responds.

"Where's Reena?" an impatient Daryl cuts to the chase and asks.

Devon and Daryl seek out their parents faces for a clue and find none. Their eyes then settle on their father.

Deep down Dave feels as if his very soul is being pierced by his sons' eyes. He looks at Dorrie a moment, clears his throat, and then calmly and resolutely tells their sons, "Reena is sick."

"Sick?" the family hears a small fairy voice yell.

The family eyes are suddenly riveted on George who is having a major reaction. He jumps off the coffee cup and runs frantically about the table top screaming, "Is? Sick? Oh, my."

"No, no, George," Dave tries to calm him.

"I'm next. I'm next." George feels his forehead. "Oh, I've got a fever," he exclaims. "See? I'm sick!" George sticks out his tongue for all to see and then, THUMP, he passes out cold.

Devon and Daryl jump up from their seats screaming, "You killed him!"

Dorrie glares at Dave, "Great. Now see what you've done Mr. Psycho-Babble Degree. You've thrown the poor little fella into a panic. Could have given him a heart attack."

"Me? But, I only."

"I'll handle this, Mr. Psychologist," Dorrie responds ignoring his weak attempt at an apology. George is receiving priority treatment. She lightly nudges the stout fairy with her index finger while softly repeating his name several times.

Dave throws his hands up in the air and pushes his chair back from the table. "I knew I should have left this for you to deal with."

Dorrie glares at him. "Sure, make a mess of a simple thing and leave it for me to clean it up."

"That's not fair," Dave defends himself.

Dorrie responds emphatically, "Maybe not, but it is true and you cannot deny that."

George slowly regains consciousness. He lies still looking around him then sits up. Totally disoriented he asks, "Did I die?"

Dorrie extends her pinky finger for George to grab. She pulls lightly helping him stand. "No, George. You didn't die, you're not even sick."

"Whew!" George is momentarily relieved. His mind quickly returns to the original subject, Reena. "But, but what about Reena?" his woeful eyes search Dave's and Dorrie's.

Dave leans across the table toward George, "She'll be back when she gets well. Maybe in a few days. We don't know yet. Reena is being treated for her problem."

George is lost in thought a moment then nods knowingly. "Yeah, cleaning. I mean, I've told her a million times being a fairy isn't so bad. But, oh no, she always has to clean everything. Wants to be like Grams. Spotless, everything always has to be spotless. And, might I mention in its place."

"George," Dave draws George's attention.

"Yes," George answers distracted by his own thoughts.

"It was a wine problem," Dave clarifies.

Now the stout fairy is confused, "Huh? Reena doesn't whine or snivel."

The boys laugh.

"Sons," Dave corrects them.

"Sorry, Dad," Devon offers.

Dorrie nudges Dave. She takes over explaining the issue to George and the boys, "Wine, as in drinking?"

"Oh, I see. Gram's juice," George responds.

"Gram's juice?" Dorrie asks in disbelief, her voice trailing off.

"Mm. Juice in bottles as Grams would say."

Dorrie and Dave's eyes meet. They suddenly realize why Grams was always so secretive about what was in her cup especially in the evenings. She would never let either of them get her a refill or carry the empty cup to the sink when she was finished. Not even when she was ill.

"Oh. Grams," Dorrie comments under her breath. She looks at Dave, "That's why she always kept her cup separate from everyone else's."

"What Mom?" Daryl asks having overheard only a snippet of his parents' conversation.

Dorrie clears her throat and continues, "As I was going to say, wine isn't juice in bottles."

Devon is confused, "You and Dad drink wine."

Daryl pipes up, "Yah. Sturgeon General says it's okay."

Dorrie looks at the table and then at the boys. She is at a loss for words. A double standard has never been her intent as a mother and it definitely is not what she ever wants to represent to their sons.

Dave clears his throat, "That's different. An occasional glass is fine. But, Reena has far more than an occasional glass. She drinks until she is too sick to do anything but sleep. Plus, she looks dreadful afterward and feels the same way."

"She can't tell herself no," Dorrie adds.

"Oh," Devon's face drops.

"It made her really sick," Dave tells them.

"Oh, no," the boys exchange worried looks between themselves and George.

George touches his lips with his index finger. He contemplates all of this for a bit then comes up with what to him is a brilliant solution, "No more Gram's juice for Reena."

Dave and Dorrie smile. They are relieved the little fellow has come to the same conclusion as they have.

"That's right," Dorrie tells him.

Mother Séance has a rude awakening not long after she drifts back to sleep. And, the thanks go to the detoxifying Reena's foul temperament. She hears banging and clattering and Reena's voice from the other room.

Pulling herself out of bed, she asks herself, "What are you doing, Reena?" This is a question she really does not want the answer to.

The little fairy knocks over the chairs, pulls books off the bookshelves, and yanks the beaded curtains to the floor. Not even the crystal ball is safe as it topples off the table and rolls onto the floor.

Mother Séance enters the room to find Reena peering under a corner of the area rug looking for an escape hatch.

"When you're done."

Startled by Mother Séance, Reena flies up to the ceiling. She takes refuge on the top of a ceiling fan blade.

"As I was saying. When you are done, you will clean up this mess." Mother Séance gathers up her crystal ball then storms out of the room.

Reena is oblivious to whatever it was Mother Séance had said. She is mesmerized by the room spinning beneath her. Oh, she suddenly does not feel well. Her complexion begins to take on a green tint.

Reena grabs her stomach and doubles over. Stars fill her eyes. She blinks and rolls off the blade flying erratically downward to the table. Splat! Reena lands on the table in a most ungracious manner.

With breakfast and the family meeting over with, the Sams' family prepares for another day. Dave finishes the last of his coffee while Dorrie packs the boys' lunch sacks.

Devon and Daryl, now dressed in school clothes, push and shove each other as they descend the stairs.

George is nowhere to be seen. He sits alone on the attic's window sill preoccupied with thoughts of the future and what will become of him, them. What if Reena does not get well? What if Reena gets well and decides she does not wish to come back here? What ifs fill his mind.

George's eyes stare blankly at the doll house in the corner of the room. It takes the better part of an hour for him to work through his thoughts, to realize his eyes are seeing something real. He sighs then slowly flies over to investigate that object in the corner of the room.

"Nice features," he admits to himself hovering at the front door.

George glances behind him to make sure he is not seen. He then cautiously, slowly pulls on the doll house's front door. To his amazement it opens. He enters.

"Oh, it's wonderful!" he exclaims.

Back at Mother Séance's shop, Reena's eyes are bloodshot. Her hair is in disarray. She trembles violently. Her skin is clammy and she sweats profusely.

Mother Séance leaves the room and returns with a handkerchief in her hand. "Poor dear."

Reena can barely focus on the source of the voice.

"It will be all right," Mother Séance tells her gently wrapping the handkerchief around her.

Reena is too sick to resist.

"You have begun to sweat the poisons from your system."

Reena cannot understand the meaning of what Mother Séance has just said to her. A full blown, throbbing headache is now waging war inside her skull and interferes with her hearing.

"I'll be right back. Going to get you some hot tea," Mother Séance steps away from Reena.

"Did she say hot tea?" Reena is so miserable feeling she cannot be sure.

A few minutes later Mother Séance returns. In her hand is a cup of tea. She spoons a bit of it out and offers it to Reena.

Reena's eyes cross as she tries to focus. But, then, she does not need her vision for this. Her sense of smell is beginning to function again. "Tea?" she screams in a hoarse voice.

"Yes, little one."

Reena weakly raises her fist and curses slurred, angry words in response. Oh, the insult. Does she not understand that Reena is Irish, not English? Does she not know American history? The Americans were the ones who dumped the tea in the harbor during the Revolutionary War. What on earth is the matter with this gypsy? An Irish fairy loathes tea. And, she, Reena, being an Irish fairy therefore also loathes tea. Drinking dirty sock water would be a preferable beverage to this fairy's way of thinking.

***

Five weeks pass with no major events occurring with the Sams' family. Everything has settled into a routine. Dorrie's mourning of Grams' has transitioned through to the final stage; that being the acceptance of Grams' death.

George has been given a place within the family unit and has been enjoying the acknowledgment and benefits of being part of the family. He is included in the household's activities just as Dave and Dorrie do with their own children.

Reena is still absent from the household, though. And George, primarily, still misses her very much. There is not a day that passes that he does not think of her and wonders how she is doing.

After Reena's first few days at Mother Séance's shop, Dave, Dorrie, and Mother Séance recognized that they needed to temporarily break communications; suspend the couple's almost daily visits. This was due to Reena's refusal to cooperate with her rehabilitation.

Each time Dave and Dorrie had contact with Reena, the little fairy stopped dealing with the real issue, being in rehabilitation for her alcoholism. Instead, she fancied the Sams' apologizing profusely and compensating her in an unrealistic manner for "their" unforgivable behavior towards her and, of course, the couple would then beg her to leave Mother Séance's shop and return to "her" home.

But, each visit ended the same. The Sams' would return home and Reena was left behind with Mother Séance. Within moments of their exit, Reena would act out in a very destructive fairylike manner; tossing furniture and the like.

It was not an easy decision for the Sams come to. To deny Reena all contact with the family caused them great anxiety but they realized it was a necessary step for her if she were to ever achieve success in rehabilitation.

Days passed between the Sams' last visit and Reena's acknowledgement that she had no choice but to deal with her problem. It was the only solution if she ever wanted to regain her freedom and return to the Sams' household.

In the weeks that followed, Mother Séance made some real headway in Reena's rehabilitation. The delirium tremens which the little fairy experienced had finally passed. Her skin color improved and her eyes regained their sparkle especially during her mischievous moments.

As I said, here it is Friday evening, the conclusion of week five. The family is gathered at the table enjoying their dinner of biscuits, gravy, vegetables, and fried chicken. (George just loves biscuits and gravy.)

George is seated in what has become his normal seating for a dinner meal, on the edge of Daryl's plate.

This meal has been unusually quiet. Everyone has been eating and there have been no conversations of school or work or household or anything. This is totally out of norm for the Sams'.

Dave looks around the table. He tries to make eye contact with the boys and then with Dorrie. No one pays him any heed. Life is taking on a monotonous routine that he finds himself hard pressed to deal with. More and more he misses some of the excitement the twins use to bring into their lives on a daily basis.

Life was anything but dull. But, of course, that was also during the time frame when their father was seldom around. A father's presence in a home can change a great many things, including a child's behavior.

"I'll call her tomorrow," Dave finally speaks up breaking the silence.

Dorrie, the boys, and George suddenly look at him leaving him with a feeling of awkwardness.

"Who?" Daryl asks.

Dorrie looks at Daryl and then at Dave, "Thank you. I don't know how much more of this I can stand." She too somewhat misses the days of uproar.

George is oblivious to everything. As usual when there is food in the area he tunes out all else. He reaches over and scoops up a handful of biscuit crumbs.

Daryl is busy trying to figure out what his parents are talking about and is inattentive to George. The result, he almost spears the stout fairy with his fork.

"I say!" George suddenly yells struggling to free his tailcoat which is pinned by the fork.

Daryl quickly moves his fork and apologizes, "Oh, George, sorry."

George dusts off his coat and looks at Daryl out of the corner of his eye.

"What?" Daryl asks him.

George pretends bashfulness, "One would think that if one were truly sorry then one might offer a payment of, say, chicken."

Dave and Dorrie watch the interaction with amusement.

"You drive a hard bargain there, George," Dave remarks.

Daryl moves several slivers of chicken over for George. "There."

George, believing that he is the supreme negotiator, nods in agreement with Dave's words.

"That's why he sits on Daryl's plate and not mine," Devon eyes the fairy.

George munching on the chicken, smiles at Devon. "That is why I would not allow myself to sit on your plate."

A few moments pass as the family finishes their dinner.

"Are you going to be home early again in the near future?" Dorrie asks Dave.

"Far more regularly than in recent years," Dave shares with her.

"Nice," she smiles.

"But, you know at some point I may have to stay late to tutor or review test results or something professorish."

"I know. But, until then, I won't miss those days at all."

"Me either," Dave winks at her.

The telephone rings, which is not an unusual evening occurrence in the Sams' household. Typically it will have something to do with the college, either a student seeking after class time help or a fellow professor wanting to discuss their day.

"Ignore it," Dave tells Dorrie.

Not answer a ringing telephone? Dorrie cannot bring herself to do that, "What if it's an emergency?"

This response makes absolutely no sense to Dave since all the family is gathered at the dining room table. "Suit yourself," he resigns himself to the fact that she will answer it regardless of what he says if for no other reason than curiosity.

Dorrie takes the call in the other room. She talks in a hushed voice to ensure no one overhears the subject of the conversation.

Daryl scoops up a spoonful of gravy and offers it to George.

George stares at it, sniffs it, dips his finger in it for a taste test, and then smiles.

"I think he likes it," Dave comments.

George wolfs the gravy in record time.

"He does," Daryl smiles.

"That little guy sure has a hearty appetite," Dave observes. "What does he have a bottomless pit for a stomach?"

George looks across the table at Dave and winks. Translation, yes he does.

Dorrie hangs up the telephone totally excited. This is probably the best news the family has had all year. She immediately goes to the kitchen. Every cupboard, especially the wine cooler, is double checked. There is absolutely no wine in the house. What a wonderful relief she feels.

Dave watches her busily move about. His curiosity piques, "You okay over there?"

Dorrie's face beams.

"I take it that means yes," Dave remarks.

Dorrie scurries back to the table. She is so excited she cannot sit down.

"So, what has you so wound up?"

Dorrie paces near the table, "You will not believe who just called."

"How many guesses do I get?" Dave jokes.

"Oh, hon," Dorrie's spirit is a little dampened.

"There's no school this week," Daryl volunteers.

"Uh, no," both parents answer simultaneously.

Dave smiles, "That was the I.R.S. calling to say that we don't owe any taxes this year."

"Honestly, Dave," Dorrie responds.

George suddenly jumps off Daryl's plate. He loves games, especially guessing games, and wants so much to participate. But, no one in the family notices him running about on the table top. So, he begins to jump up and down while waving emphatically.

Dave tries again and offers, "I've been offered a huge pay increase?"

"Don't be ridiculous," Dorrie shakes her head.

George is getting winded. He gasps trying to catch his breath and thereby draws Dorrie's attention.

"George?"

One should understand that by the time he has a chance to be heard, George is no longer in the mood. His energy is spent. Now all he wants is the answer. "I say," he says between pants. "I would think that perhaps you should just tell us."

"Good idea, George. Hon, just tell us," Dave suggests. The suspense of what the news could be is getting to all of them, even him.

Dorrie stops. She looks each member of her family in the eyes a thoughtful moment. "Well," she says very slowly allowing the suspense to mount. "That phone call was about," Dorrie stops and walks around to the other side of the table, again for dramatic effect.

"Dorrie," Dave's patience is beginning to wear thin.

"Hm?" she looks at him as though she has no clue as to what could possibly be bothering him. She smiles with the grin of a Cheshire cat, "Reena. She's coming home soon."

The boys and George let out loud cheers at the top of their lungs.

Dave chokes on his coffee. "That's good," he says hesitantly. There is no way he will know until the time comes if Reena will retaliate for the vacuum cleaner trip to Mother Séance's.

"This is cause for celebration," George announces.

"Yes, it is," Dorrie agrees.

In the next instant, George leaps upward and dives head first into the gravy dish. This is his version of taking a "victory" lap as one would in a swimming pool.

"Eugh!" Dorrie turns her head.

The boys burst out in laughter. Dave stifles his own.

"Anything we need to do before she gets here?" Dave asks.

"Huh, oh, I don't think so."

"When is she coming?" Daryl wants to know. Heck they all want to know.

"In a few days. I imagine Mother Séance will call us before she heads out," Dorrie tells them.

***

Within 72 hours of receiving the news about Reena's completion of rehabilitation at Mother Séance's shop, the Sams' family gathers in the foyer. Today is the day of her homecoming. And, they are all quite eager to welcome the rehabilitated Reena home, especially the George. After all, in the many years they have spent together, they had never been separated before this twist of fate.

"This is a big day for all of us," Dave acknowledges.

Dorrie nods. "Hon, do you think she remembers how she got to Mother Séance's shop?" she whispers to her husband. It appears that Dave is not the only one concerned with Reena's possibly reprisal.

Dave nervously adjusts his shirt collar, "I hope not."

"Me too."

The family hears a vehicle pull up in front of their house.

"She's here!" Devon and Daryl announce excitedly.

Dave steps up to the door. "Boys, give Mother Séance a chance to enter the house, okay?"

"Yah," they respond totally distracted.

Dave catches a look at the type of vehicle one gypsy, Mother Séance, might be driving. To his amusement he sees a psychedelic van. "Might of known," he mumbles to himself.

The van door squeaks loudly when Mother Séance opens it and she must slam it to get it to close all the way. Dave watches and listens chuckling quietly to himself.

Mother Séance slowly approaches the Sams' front door with a small box. Just as she nears the door, she stops a moment and pats the small box that is tightly clutched under her arm. "Almost there, Reena. You're almost home."

Reena sits in a corner of the box, cross-legged. The last time she went anywhere and it involved the Sams' or Mother Séance for that matter, the outcome was definitely not to her liking. She has no real desire to find out what will actually lie on the other side of this box if and when it should open.

With fist poised to knock, Mother Séance finds the door suddenly opens wide for her. Her knuckles never make contact with the door.

The boys immediately scurry away from the window and despite his best effort they are the first to greet the gypsy. "Wow, a gypsy!" they say in wide-eyed wonder. Prior to this they thought that gypsies were only in books.

Dave extends his hand, "Mother Séance, please come in. Please don't mind the boys. They do know their manners even though they do not always practice them."

"Thank you. I'd forgotten what a lovely home this is."

George stops himself short choosing to hover behind a plant in the corner. He remembers Mother Séance from a long, long time ago.

"Forgotten?" Dave asks.

"Hm?" Mother Séance realizes she has had a slip of the tongue and that she must be mindful not to validate what she had just said.

Dave looks over to Dorrie to see if perhaps she had also heard Mother Séance. It is obvious from her expression that she has not.

Mother Séance takes a few steps into the foyer being mindful to keep the box tucked safely under her arm.

The twins immediately crowd around her. Try as they may, they cannot get even the slightest peek of the contents held with the confines of that small box in her possession.

"Where's Reena?" Daryl, having no patience, is first to ask.

"She's right here," Mother Séance softly pats the box.

George scowls. "Reena in a box? Oh, not good, not good."

"She's fine now?" asks Dave.

Mother Séance nods. "For the most part."

Dorrie whispers to Dave, "For the most part? That doesn't sound good."

Mother Séance overhears Dorrie's concern. "I'll explain in a minute. The poor dears want to see their fairy," she smiles warmly at the twins.

"Oh, yeah," the boys say in unison.

"Boys," Dave motions for the boys to step back. "Give Mother Seance a little breathing room."

Mother Séance waves Dave off. She speaks to Devon and Daryl, "Oh, that's quite all right. I would be excited too if I were them, waiting on a fairy."

Dorrie steps up. "You can set it on the table if you'd like," she indicates the table.

"All right."   Mother Séance sets the box down and quickly steps back.   "I imagine little Reena is more than ready to exit her mode of transportation. I had a dickens of a time getting her in there this morning." She shakes her head at the memory.

"Really. How did you manage it?" Dave asks.

"She was sleeping when I made the transfer."

"And, she woke up to find herself in a box?" Dorrie asks concerned with Reena's reaction.

"Oh, definitely, not good," sweat now beads on George's brow. "What a heathen," he snarls at Mother Séance.

"Unfortunately, Reena still has a bit of a stubborn streak so I had to do what it took to get her here," Mother Séance says with a tinge of sadness in her voice. "She should understand though."

"We hope," Dave says dreading Reena's reaction when she is set free of her confines.

"Can we open the box now, Dad?" Devon asks.

"In a moment.   There is something I need to have clarified with Mother Séance first. Just a couple of more minutes."

"Ah, Dad," the boys whine.

George moves to the front of the plant. He hovers just behind Mother Séance. No one pays him any heed. It is as though he is invisible.

Dorrie and Dave sidle up to Mother Séance.   Dave speaks first, "What is it you were going to tell us?"

"Um?" Mother Séance is distracted by the boys.

"She's fine for the most part, right?" Dorrie inserts.

"Oh, yes, pretty much."

"Pretty much?" Dave questions.

Mother Séance lowers her voice so the boys do not overhear her. "It's juice. Reena still seems to have a bit of a problem understanding the difference between wine and juice, grape juice actually."

"A bit of a problem? Just how big of a bit is it?" Dave is skeptical.

Mother Séance would really prefer to avoid this subject but it must be said. Sooner or later the family would find out anyway that her detoxification of Reena was not as successful as they had all hoped, "From Reena's perspective wine and juice, grape juice, are the same."

"They're what?" Dave asks in disbelief.

"She doesn't know the difference?" Dorrie follows with her own question.

"But, I'm sure that with the passage of time and the absence of that particular type of juice she will be fine. After all, she has been dry for several weeks now."

"Good," Dorrie says with hesitation.

Mother Séance looks at the boys and then at Dave and Dorrie, "If you've no further questions or concerns, I really need to rush off. I have another appointment."

"Sure," Dorrie responds.

Dave smiles, "Another fairy?"

"No," Mother Séance chuckles. "A gnome."

"Oh." Dave suddenly feels foolish. He should have known not to ask.

"Dad," Daryl pleads.

Mother Séance asks, "It's all right for them to open the box now?"

"We were thinking of letting you do the honors," Dave winks.

"Oh, no. I put her in there and I'm sure I'm the last person she wants to see right now."

"You're probably right about that," Dave smiles.

"Dad?" the boys impatiently call him.

"The great unveiling," Dave thinks to himself.

"Oh, Dave," Dorrie is tired of the suspense.

Devon and Daryl jockey for position at the box. It will actually only take one of them to open it.

She tells the boys, "You can open the box any time."

The boys have the box top removed before the words finish crossing her lips.

Reena, sitting in a corner of her confines, has felt another slight jostling of the box. She ignores it the way she has ignored all of them since her rude awakening to this cardboard prison.

Daryl and Devon cannot believe their eyes. They look at each other and then at Reena several times. Seconds turn into minutes and yet, the fairy does not move. The twins were definitely expecting an entirely different reaction from Reena; one of immediate flight.

"She's not moving," Daryl cries.

George is alarmed. He flies directly over to Reena and hovers above the box. "Reena?" he says expecting recognition. But, there is none. George looks up at the boys. His eyes pleading for help.

Devon motions for George to back away. "I'll get it," he tells George.

Daryl anxiously watches his brother put his index finger in the box.

There is no reaction from Reena.

Both boys scream, "Mom!"

Dorrie, Dave, and Mother Séance pass troubled looks to each other.

"I, I don't understand," Mother Séance says.

"She's probably upset, boys," Dave informs the twins.

Mother Séance turns toward the door. "Perhaps she is upset with me and will venture out of the box once I leave."

Dorrie and Dave find this a reasonable explanation.

"You're probably right. Let me get the door for you," Dave opens the door.

"Call me if her attitude does not change."

"Right," Dorrie responds.

"Mom, Dad," the boys call their parents in unison.

"Just a minute sons. Say goodbye to Mother Séance. She has to leave now," Dorrie tries to encourage the boys to remember their manners.

"Yah, bye," Devon snaps.

"Enjoy your fairy," Mother Séance steps out the door.

Reena suddenly hears it. It finally sinks in that the voice she has been hearing belongs to that awful gypsy. Shock registers on her face. She is suddenly jolted out of her catatonic-like state. The little fairy leaves the confines of the box like a heat-seeking missile.

"Mom, Dad, look!" Daryl calls.

Dave barely manages to close the front door just in time to keep Reena separated from Mother Séance.

George zips around the room. He is so ecstatic to have his friend back that he does not know what to do first.

Reena comes to a screeching halt a few inches shy of the door. She spins about and glares at Dave. Her eyes narrow and she makes faces at him.

"I think that answers the question as to whether or not she is upset," Dave comments.

The boys laugh. George hovers in the corner.

A moment passes.

"Reena," Dorrie scolds the ungrateful fairy. "Mother Séance helped you."

Reena mimics Dorrie.

"Stop it," Dave commands her. "You need to learn some manners."

"Not good, not good, this is so not good," George covers his eyes. He cannot bear to watch.

"Huh?" Reena says to Dave with a smile.

"Reena, that is absolutely shameful behavior," Dorrie adds.

Reena's brow rises. A determined look washes over her face. She and Dorrie make brief eye contact. Reena winks at her and immediately begins mimicking Dorrie's walk.

"Why you little," Dorrie is insulted.

Reena points, laughs, and then flies out of the room with the boys and George in pursuit.

Dave just stands there mute silent waiting for everyone to clear the foyer. Once they are gone he looks up at the ceiling and shakes his head, "Grams, I owe you one."

Reena's madly dashes through every room of the house. She is truly enjoying the freedom of flight back in "her" house, even if she has to share it with these people.

Each room is briefly inspected by Reena for any changes the Sams' family may have made during her absence. She is quite pleased to find there are none, at least not in the downstairs areas.

"Reena," George is quite winded. He had forgotten how much faster she can fly than he. Not to mention how much further she can fly.

Reena slows a moment. It is just enough to allow her friend to catch up to her. "Yes?" she asks as if he has deterred her from some great mission.

"The attic." Those are the only words George has an opportunity to say to her before she takes off again.

Up the stairs she goes with George and the twins in pursuit.

Dave and Dorrie slowly bring up the rear. They want to see Reena's reaction to the fairies' new home without interfering with them.

"Reena!" Daryl suddenly calls out.

Reena comes to a fast stop. She turns to look behind her. It then dawns on her that from the moment she left the foyer she has been oblivious to the boys and their parents. "Grief," she moans. "Go away."

"Okay," Devon calmly responds to Daryl's dismay.

In the moments that Reena's entry into the attic was stalled, George was able to sneak past her. This opportunity allows him to be at their new house before she sees it.

Reena spins about thinking the boys are a bothersome lot. She happily flies into the attic finding nothing out of place. And, then, she sees it. Surely her eyes deceive her. She blinks, not once or twice but several times.

"Oh, this is going to be so good," Daryl excitedly whispers.

"Oh, yah," Devon agrees.

"It's ours," George calls to Reena.

Reena is shocked, dismayed, confused, ecstatic, and at a total loss for words.

"It's our new home," George opens the front door.

Reena slowly approaches. Her eyes are as big as saucers taking in the many details of the home's exterior. "Ours?" she asks in disbelief.

"Ours," George affirms.

One by one, Reena tests all the doors and windows, opening and closing each one. Her hands run along the draperies and the furniture inside as well. This is real furniture not a matchbox stuffed with cotton. It has a real kitchen complete with pots and pans and utensils and a working stove and refrigerator and sink, and, and, Reena is truly overwhelmed.

"Oh," she keeps saying over and over in total in wonder at its many luxuries.

"Well, hon, I think she really likes it," Dave wraps his arm around Dorrie's shoulder.

"Let's give them some time to get reacquainted with each other," Dorrie suggests to the boys.

The boys leave but not without first voicing their objections, "Do we have to?"

Dave looks sternly at his sons. "Yes."

***

Reena's first day back has been one of excitement for everyone but most especially her. The now nearly exhausted fairy has spent almost the entire day in flight. Not wanting to rest nor slow down. How her wings missed their exercise. They had felt so cramped at Mother Séance's shop.

There was no place to go. There were no multiple rooms, no flights of stairs, and no attic. The shop is one-tenth the size of this house. Oh, yes, how she missed the space.

When evening comes Reena finds that tonight has been designated a special occasion. Dave and Dorrie have taken great effort at ensuring it is celebrated much like one would a family reunion. There are welcome home signs hanging from the doorways and helium filled balloons drifting through several rooms of the house.

And, what would a proper celebration be if it does not, of course, include a multiple course dinner meal consisting of the family's and fairies' favorite foods. It is a rather decadent spread designed to please everyone's palate. Which it does.

After dinner everyone pitches in to clean up the dishes and pots and pans. The fairies transport the utensils to the sink, the boys take the plates, and Dave gets the glasses. Everyone helps at placing all the leftovers in appropriate storage containers for the refrigerator. The dishwasher is filled and the countertops and table are wiped down.

"Guess we're ready to retire to the living room?" Dave kisses Dorrie on the cheek.

"Retire?" Daryl asks.

Dorrie smiles, "That means watch a movie or something."

"Then why didn't Dad say that?" Daryl shrugs and walks away.

Dorrie and Dave follow their sons toward the kitchen door leading to the living room. They notice that Reena is not in the group.

Devon turns, his eyes roam the kitchen, "Where's Reena?"

"Well, I don't..." Dorrie's voice trails off when she sees Reena hovering in the center of the kitchen. "That's odd."

Reena floats in the middle of the room. She looks it over several times and then begins to fly in a pattern indicative of having lost something.

"What's she doing?" Dave asks Dorrie.

Dorrie shrugs, "Maybe she is just happy to be here."

Dave laughs, "Or hungry like her buddy, George."

Devon and Daryl who left the kitchen a few moments earlier return.

"Have you seen George?" Daryl asks.

Reena stops. She cocks her head, stares at the boys. What a relief to know she is not the only one who has misplaced her stout friend.

"No. Thought he was with you," Dave answers.

The boys shake their heads.

"He was still here when we left the kitchen," Devon explains.

Dorrie stares over at Reena, "That explains what's going on with Reena."

"You're probably right," responds Dave.

Reena suddenly flies up to the refrigerator. She hovers a moment then presses her ear into the door.

"Ah, you don't think?" Dorrie casts a concerned look at Dave.

Dave shakes his head, "He does love food."

Reena withdraws her ear from the refrigerator and backs away. A mild spin on her part and the door swings open. She squeals.

Sitting in a slouched position in an empty pie dish is George. A very full and cold, George.

Dave and Dorrie rush up to the refrigerator followed by the twins. Dave reaches into the refrigerator and quickly pulls out the dish with the seated George on board.

"Did you get enough sweet potato pie, George?" he asks the fairy.

George smiles then burps.

"I'll take it that means yes."

Reena approaches George. Her hands go on her hips and she begins chattering at a speed none of them have ever heard before. This is fairy language for "George is receiving a good scolding". Moments later she is silent.

"So sorry," they hear George apologize. He really is sorry. Mostly sorry for having been caught by Reena. As for the pie, not so much. It was quite delicious.

Reena shakes her head.

"That's all right, George," Dorrie offers. "Just next time be more careful."

"Yes, mum," George tips his hat in true gentleman style.

Reena takes his hand and helps him out of the dish.

It must have been the compression of air in his system that causes a burp far larger than he is tall to suddenly erupt. He quickly covers his mouth, a tad bit embarrassed, "Sorry again."

"I'm glad you enjoyed your dinner, George," Dorrie says putting the dish in the dishwasher.

"Sounds like he's still enjoying is," Devon laughs.

George looks at the family one at a time then confesses, "I say, I think that delicious pie ran away with my common sense."

Dave asks Dorrie, "Are we done in the kitchen now?"

Dorrie rinses her hands in the sink then dries them, "Yes."

"Dave, mister, sir, Sams'," George still has yet to decide what he should call him.

"Yes, George?" Dave responds. "You can call me Dave or Mr. Sams."

"We call him dad," Daryl offers.

"Yes, well, Mr. Dave, mm, might I say," everyone's eyes are on George. "You might want to turn the heat up in that thing. It is awfully cold." George informs them matter-of-factly.

Dave shakes his head, "That's why they call it a refrigerator. It's supposed to be cold."

"I see." George begins to ponder how he might best survive such chilly conditions. It only makes sense, right? That since the best food in the house is in the refrigerator, then that's where he should get his meals, dine in other words. (You see these fairies have no experience, no knowledge of fairy parkas).

"Now that the great mystery as to George's whereabouts has been resolved I think tonight I'll read a book." Dave looks at the twins, "What do you say?"

"What kind of book?" Devon wants to know before answering his father.

"You'll see."

Devon persists, "But, I might have read it."

"Not this one, you wouldn't have," Dave has a doubtful look on his face. "Is there something you want to watch on television?"

Devon quickly offers, "No." There truly is but he knows his father would not approve. It is a modern day crime show and according to his father there is too much violence in it.

"Good," his father responds.

Now, during Reena's weeks of absence out of the household, Dave and Dorrie had designated one evening each week as family night. This special time was reserved for Dave to either read a book to the boys and George (of course they would not exclude the stout fairy) or they would all enjoy a good family oriented movie.

The object of family night has been successful at helping to repair the strained relationships between Dave and Dorrie and between Dave and his sons; bonding as some would say. Even George has benefited from these evenings. He just loves picture shows as he calls them.

Reena's return to this family has introduced her to a whole different environment than the one she had left. This is a much better place than before. The little fairy has busily taken mental notes all the positive differences in the family; Dave is no longer "owned" by his employer and Dorrie's once frayed nerves have been replaced with a much calmer and even tempered disposition.

Reena has also noted that Devon and Daryl's moments of discord are not nearly to the degree they once were. And, George, he has developed greater self-confidence and is no longer as easily frightened.

George's greatest role in the household centers on the kitchen (naturally). It evolved as a result of Dorrie's observation that the stout fairy has a far better sense of taste when it comes to selecting which foods compliment each other. Plus, as an added bonus he is absolutely fantastic at helping her with seasonings and spices at mealtime and he is a wonderful little taste tester.

Reena follows the family into the living room unsure as to what she should expect. So, she tails George at what she figures is a discreet distance. Within a few minutes of entering the living room she faces the realities of just how deeply rooted the changes in the Sams' home life are.

Dave is first to enter the living room. There is a special book he pulled from the bookshelf prior to dinner that he intends to read to the twins and the fairies. And, he wants this book to be a surprise for them so he slid it out of view underneath the sofa.

The boys automatically sit on the sofa leaving a space for their father to sit between them. George flies up and hovers over the sofa waiting for Dave to be seated. Reena cocks her head, her interest is piqued.

Dave picks up the book and sits between the twins. He starts to open the book when George clears his throat. Dave nonchalantly looks at the fairy, "Yes, George?"

George is confused. He looks at the book then at Dave and then winces.

Dave smiles, "George, you know I won't start the book till you take your seat. And, Reena too. She is invited just as you are."

With that said, George happily perches himself on Dave's right shoulder. Reena, following him, is diverted to Dave's left shoulder by George.

Well, now that Devon, Daryl, Reena, and George are seated with Dave on the sofa he lets them see the book he has chosen. As he had hoped, it is definitely a pleasant surprise for them all.

"And so the story begins," Dave starts to read.

Reena almost slides off his shoulder. What is it she sees that is drawing her attention so dramatically? Why it is none other than pictures of fairies; fairies from other cultures, lands, countries. There are short ones and tall ones and fat ones and thin ones and even a bald one. She giggles at the sight of that last one.

Dorrie sits in a chair near the kitty-corner to the sofa. Her head rests on the back of the chair and she closes her eyes. These evenings are so relaxing and bring back such good memories from when she was a child and was read to by her own parents.

Dave spends a few minutes reading the captions beneath the pictures on the pages he has already read.

"Hon," Dorrie says softly.

Dave looks up from the book. It must be bedtime for the twins. Dorrie would not interrupt a reading otherwise. He slips a bookmark the book so he will know where he left off.

"Well, sad to say but it is bedtime everyone," he says to the boys and the fairies.

"Oh, Dad," the boys protest.

Sighs are also heard from the fairies.

"I say I find this a most interesting book," George shares.

"Yeah, Dad, what he said," Daryl adds.

"Well in that case I guess we will just have to finish reading this book tomorrow," Dave promises closing the book.

Dave's promise to return to the book tomorrow night meets with the boys and the fairies satisfaction.

Dorrie stands, "Off to bed guys."

Devon and Daryl slowly leave the living room. The fairies fly not far behind them.

"Look kinda cute don't they?" Dave muses. "Almost like having four children. Well, two and a tenth children."

"Oh, Dave," Dorrie laughs lightly.

"If you hadn't drifted off to sleep, Dad would have kept reading," Devon accuses Daryl.

"Did not."

"Did too."

Devon and Daryl begin shoving each other up the staircase.

Reena taps George on the shoulder then a slightly wicked smile traces across her face.

George shakes his head in disapproval.

Reena flies up behind Devon (her least favorite of the twins) and sharply yanks his hair.

"Ouch!" Devon yells. "Stop that!"

Reena darts in front of Devon, "Make me!"

Devon makes a made dash up the last couple of steps only to find Reena is nowhere in sight.

"Boys!" they hear their father's voice. "Go straight to bed."

"You know those boys were good all day," Dorrie sighs.

Dave smiles, "They just can't seem to make it through an entire day without some form of an eruption."

"At least it not as bad as it use to be."

"Not as bad," Dave repeats.

Dave and Dorrie suddenly hear Devon's voice echoing loudly. It is as if his vocal chords are transcending the very walls of the house, "Reena, stop it!"

Dave cuts his laugh short. "Reena, straight to bed," he calls after the little rabble rouser.

"You are disciplining Reena now, too?" Dorrie asks in disbelief. "It's her first day home. Wouldn't it be better to give her a few days to adjust to the changes around here?"

Dave makes eye contact with her and pulls her onto his lap. "Well, hon, this is the way I see it. Remember how you use to wonder what it would be like if the boys had a little sister?"

"Yes. But what does that have to do with this?"

"I think now that Reena is back in the household you just may very well find out the answer to that question. And, I also think that tonight is only the beginning."

Dorrie shakes her head. She had never even remotely considered Reena or George as surrogate children or having delinquent behaviors. That is not until now. Dave has thrown a new perspective on the twins, fairies issue.

"Ready to go to bed?" Dave kisses her on the cheek.

"In a moment." Dorrie's hand touches the book, "Where did you ever find this book?"

"I think it was in a little shop in town. Give me a minute to remember," he thoughtfully strokes his brow.

Dorrie mocks, "There are only two shops in our town."

"Ah, yes, Mother Séance. I do believe her name was Mother Séance."

Dorrie picks the book up and holds it a moment before setting it down. "Interesting title, 'A Dusty Tale'.

"I thought so. There is supposed to be a series of them. Don't know if they are all about fairies."

And so the story ends.......
                    for now......

CONTACT INFORMATION:

http://tindernotes.net

www.lulu.com/tinder